D

The City Man

The City Man

Howard Akler

Coach House Books

first edition

Published with the assistance of the Canada Council for the Arts and the Ontario Arts Council. We also acknowledge the Government of Ontario through the Ontario Book Publishing Tax Credit Program and the Government of Canada through the Book Publishing Industry Development Program.

LIBRARY AND ARCHIVES CANADA CATALOGUING IN PUBLICATION

Akler, Howard, 1969-
    The city man / Howard Akler.

ISBN 1-55245-158-5

    I. Title.

PS8601.K44C58 2005   C813´.6   C2005-905083-7

for Susan Kernohan

Part One

March 1934

Each minute this morning hangs perilously, like long cigarette ash. She flicks her wrist. Grey flakes fall onto the grey marble floor. All around her is the click-click of shoes and dollied steamer trunks that rumble in the rotunda of the Great Hall. Her eyes are steady. Watching intently the line of suckers at the ticket window and the bills that emerge one by one from their pockets. The first is a fiver, the next two are singles. She smiles. Sees clearly now the corner of a ten-dollar bill and leans forward, budging the moment when they will begin to head her way. She takes another drag. Tendrils of smoke curl around her hand.

Here they come.

He takes the 9:20 train from Gravenhurst. Loosens his tie, leans his forehead against the window. Reflection all the way. He sees his own eyes, the familiar expression that locomotes down rural routes, passing across farmhouses into pale flat land. Studies this face, the crow's feet and jawline that jump with each jolt of the tracks, that align themselves with the speed of the train so his mug is oddly still within the restless geography. This is how he heads home. Takes a deep breath and the blur on the other side of the window continues to accelerate. Silos blink past. Town after nameless town disintegrates behind him. Eli slouches in his red leather seat and watches each one vanish.

The train pulls into Union Station. One last jolt and he lurches out of his seat. Looks around. Passengers yawn and retrieve their hats from overhead. Jam the aisle. A welter of hips along the length of the car. Behind an angora beret, Eli takes small steps. Maunder and pause, maunder and pause. They advance tediously and then disembark, with traincases and a sigh, onto the platform. Move single file through a set of doors.

An arrant crowd on the arrivals concourse. Hustling redcaps go blue in the face, lugging huge bags in their thin arms. Around them, dozens of people offer tips and gesticulations. This way this way this way. Elbowing a path from the ramp loggia to the taxi stand. This way this way. Eli, a tight grip on his satchel, negotiates the hollering. Finds brief open spaces and makes his move, zigzagging here and there. He keeps on his toes, almost midway, when his route is cut off by a murmuring couple. He stops, steps back suddenly and bumps into an old woman. Pinched face and a scent of rosewater.

Well I never, she says.

Eli shrugs. Picks up again the circuitous pace and feels a slight dispersal in the crowd. Just stragglers now in wider spaces. Waiting and waiting, all the expectant eyes focus on the arrivals gate. For the hundredth time this hour, a cigarette is crushed under a shoe.

One level up. Light from clerestory windows cuts a series of pale lines through the crowd. A gaggle of hats and torsos gone lucent. Mona Kantor keeps watch. In all the comings and goings she can see shades of possibility. A sucker who fumbles with a street map, another dickering with smash. Her eyes all over these men, her sense of the grift roving under footfalls and around a farewell hug before hitting her mark. Six-footer in a tilted homburg, reading the frieze of destinations on the north wall of the station. Port-Arthur, North-Bay, Sarnia. His lips on the move. Mona looks to the opposite wall. Chesler, in the arranged spot, offers only hat and hands around an open newspaper. His eye rises over the corner in silent accord. He folds the paper, buries it in his armpit and steps away from the wall.

Through the bodies they move, scissoring the floor of the station. Two thieves in step with the mark, appearing casual despite the practiced footwork. A shuffling celerity. Passengers from all directions slowly clog the ramp of the departures concourse. Chesler slides in behind the tall man, a signal to Mona. She positions herself in front of the pair, just off to the left. The pace becomes languid now, each movement huddled around another. Mona removes her hat and wipes her brow. The felt hat dangles in her hand, a good grip on the brim. Her elbow in a hard angle almost touches the wrist beside her.

Chesler keeps one eye on the loose collar of the mark. The jacket is an ill fit, with a noticeable sag down the back. He coughs a gentle back-of-the-throat cough.

Mona drops her elbow, her hat shading Chesler's fingertips as they scurry along the left-hand pockets of the mark, coat and pants, fingertips so sentient they are in fleet accord with all the geometries of scratch. There is a roll of bills in the side pants pocket and a wallet in the back pants pocket. Chesler is set to cop.

Eyes forward, Mona manoeuvres the mark into a vulnerable position using her back and elbows and buttocks. Plants her prat with gestures incidental but calculated, small moves so ordinary they are overlooked. Her hip brushes the side of the mark's hand and Chesler gets his duke down, fast, hidden behind Mona's hat. With only the first two fingers, he takes pleat after pleat from the lining of the pocket, money rising into his hand with amazing speed. He reefs an easy kick, a small wad of money in his palm. Once more he coughs. Mona shortens her stride. Each step is smaller and smaller, so small the trio is both fluid and inert. The mark is dull to rhythm and he moves into her. A slight swivel of the hips for misdirection. The surest way to get a man's mind off his money is to focus on the space between the pockets. Just for one priapic moment, a sucker's epoch. Chesler unbuttons the back pocket with a flip of the first joint of the index finger and the ball of the thumb. He pinches the poke and slips out beyond the jibing bodies. The touch has come off without a flaw, a thing of beauty in twelve seconds, in a whiz.

Leaving Union Station, the taxicab struggles in the noontime traffic. Pedestrians, autos and streetcars all take turns with the lurch and idle.

Slumped in the back seat, Eli pats his breast pocket. Through the fabric of his jacket, he can feel the edge of the folded page, the slim heft of his release papers. He closes his eyes and mouths two words that are lost to a sudden honking horn. Eli opens his eyes, looks out the window. All the automobiles, the main street that disgorges more and more hustle. Three women, laughing, dodge the imbroglio and then the cab follows suit. Makes a quick right and, for the rest of the way, moves quietly through a mesh of side streets.

Garron's Smoke Shop, on College west of Bathurst. In the big store window, ads for Sweet Caporals are pasted around a selection of pipes and the florid face of Garron's missus, who waves. Eli waves back. He enters off the side and up one floor. Walks down a hallway of crumbling plaster, taking the same unhurried steps he has always taken, to the last door on the right.

Inside. He drops his satchel on the floor and makes a small circle of the apartment. One step after the other, Eli rounds the room with slowly increasing wont. He tilts his head, blinks before an old armchair. Seconds pile into minutes while he eyes a tear in the upholstery. He leans close to a nightstand, lamp with a fake pewter base. Four minutes pass by the time he continues to the kitchen, where look turns to touch. His left forefinger feels the dust-covered countertop and then runs a pale line clear across to the icebox. Up a wall. Stops on a calendar, two months out of date. Two months. Not much by the looks of it. Nothing more than a couple of pages. All the days he's been gone marked with tidy little boxes, check check check. The days counted out so effortlessly here. Not there. There, time passed only with a nurse's permission. A doctor's needle. But here, whole seasons can change with one flip of the page.

RIIIII-iip goes January. He reaches out for February now. Takes hold. RIIIII-iip! The two pieces of paper flutter down. Eli begins to catch up.

T hree more scores and they call it a day. Tough to ankle when the going is good but no point burning up the place, so with tempered desire they weave and flow with the rest of the suckers. Slow down near the exit.

Chesler is counting the cash.

Mona lights up. Well?

Mm-hmm.

What's that mean?

Means mm-hmm.

Mona takes a healthy drag. Well, she says, hand mine over then.

Chesler hands hers over.

Sunlight pale and slatted comes through the colonnade of Union Station. Dwarfed by a massive column, Mona squints out at the movement on Front Street. Even off the whiz, she is observant of gait and pace, the telltale vulnerabilities in another's motion. She takes a drag on her cigarette and looks around. Chesler is long gone, ready to breeze the moment the last poke is pinched. Mona tends to linger – daffy habit for a stall, but spending so much time in the tip often leaves her a little twitchy in the initial open spaces. So, on the peripheries of action, she smokes. Inhale and exhale easing her out of the grift.

Strolling away from the station, she passes a pencil seller on the sidewalk. Over her shoulder are a cigar shop and an oculist and competing haberdasheries. Sees familiar faces in the shop windows because she often takes the same route home, walks the relentless city while autos zip past with growling regularity. Six-cylinder hubbub. A honking Dodge hustles past her. She flips him the bird and turns onto the side streets. Beat-up rowhouses on McCaul and Sullivan, with cracked toplights and, below them, the unemployed who drowse in the doorways. She cuts across Spadina and walks one block north of Dundas to Glen Baillie Place, an alley four houses deep. She stops at the last one, tosses away her smoke and opens the door.

The next day, he leans his head back. Each new angle of the eye offers another storey, a gaze that climbs the spandrels, clambers over a dramatic setback and then a subtler one higher up the shaft. Eli at the corner of King and Bay stares up all twenty-two floors of the Star Building. Motionless on the sidewalk, but his eye wavers and wavers at the top. Tips over. A vertiginous drop all the way down to the main doors. He straightens his tie.

In he goes.

I'm talking about character. I'm talking about temperament. Christ, you know what I'm talking about: the news game is no place for nerves. You got deadline pressure, you got the goddamned *Tely* boys on your ass. You really take your licks in this business.

Eli shifts in his chair. Takes a deep breath. The entire newsroom stuffed into a single moment of respiration: the incessant clack-clack of keys, phones that ring through the blue smoke and blue language. The eyes of all the other reporters landing on him while Bert Murneau, the city editor, sits on the edge of the copy desk and sighs.

We've been friends for how long, Morenz?

Five years, says Eli.

Five years. So you won't squawk when I say this: I talked to your doctor yesterday.

Eli cocks an eyebrow.

He was a little cagey at first, but we managed to cut through a lot of the mumbo-jumbo. He says the rest did you wonders. Says you're much better. Says it's time to try the next step. Reintegration at a higher level, or something like that. Can't remember the exact phrase, but it all boils down to putting you back on the payroll.

Okay.

Of course, the payroll's just been cut. All I could wrangle for you was some voucher jobs. Nothing steady.

Okay.

Half the town's on relief, Morenz. You're lucky they even let you back here.

It's okay, Bert. Really.

Really? says Bert.

Eli taps his temple. Temperament, he says.

Back in the tip. The terminal crammed today, women and men who scurry and lug their way out of town. She sees whistles and waves; all the eddies of movement end up fifteen feet from the ticket window when a lanky bates joggles the crowd. Mona hard on his heels. Deliberate and innocuous, she needs only seconds to adjust to his loose jangly gait. Her mimicry moves from the announcement boards to the baggage check before she feels Chesler fall into place. Hears him cluck, an office that asks her to come through. So she does. Moves from the front of the mark and doubles back, a subtle reversal that opens enough space for Chesler to score the pit. Another office now, a muttered *ahem*, hits her ears and she knows they have pinched another poke.

Between scores, she wanders the terminal. Lights up.

From the Front Street portico comes an elderly couple. They shuffle along slowly, laboured breath and halting steps. As Mona settles in for the frame, she can see the old man tap his wristwatch.

Durn thing.

I told you to get it fixed.

I know.

I told you to take care of it. I told you it's no good but do you ever listen to me? Do you?

Mona plants her prat, then hears Chesler office that the touch has come off. With a sideways glance, she watches the couple nudge their way down the departure ramp, so eager to catch their train they won't savvy the lost poke until they are far out of town.

In the Bowles Lunch, where empty cups and full ashtrays cover the tables and hollow-eyed men scan the want ads in a shared newspaper. Eli, waiting here three days for his first assignment, kills time with the city news. A slow reacquaintance with stick-ups and social programs that jangles his caffeinated nerves and gives him a full-on jag by the end of page two. He takes a sip. Chews his lip. All the bunk about three squares and regular sleep plays well out in the country, but this business is something else entirely. The news game is all about questions. Not just the ones he has to ask – the whos, whats, wheres – but the ones he'll have to answer. How *are* you, Morenz? You okay, Morenz? You *okay*? Everyone at the paper has this scoop: the long days and late nights he needed to pound out copy, pages and pages of it that piled up until Eli couldn't go any further and the words began to dwindle. To die. And after a while, there was nothing left to say so he said nothing. Not a word. The doctor had a bunch of names for it. Nerve strain, melancholia, depression. Back then, Eli ignored any clinical hokum. But now, when the depressed man returns to the depressed city, his smile is thinner than a vein.

So, says Chesler. What's new?

He puts his empty glass down on the newspaper. A smidgen of moisture seeps onto the page, spreads slowly so articles dampen in increments. The police news soon blotted. Across the table is Polonsky. His big hands are dainty with the pouch of tobacco. He rolls two cigarettes with delicate languor.

Polonsky sips his drink. Was bumping gums with Cobourg Henry, he says. Remember him? Always in over his head. We used to work the hotel hustle, y'know. King Eddy, Royal York. And we angle this bates one day. A jug touch for sure, don't even have to fan the guy to know he's fat. So I'm fronting for Henry. And the kid's thinking he's a cannon and a half.

Daisy Medwick walks over with fresh drinks, bracelets clinking on both wrists. Her skin like old vanilla pudding, hair petrified by years of henna. Daisy was a choice stall in her day, hustling with a retinue of old-time cannons: Fishkin, Erlich, Applebaum. Now her arthritic fingers are barely nimble enough to open a bottle, pour a shot. Most of the mockies on the whiz punch gun in her place, a living-room speak in a two-storey house on Glen Baillie. Rooms rented upstairs.

She slides in beside Polonsky.

Give me a puff, baby, won't you? she says and Polonsky passes her the cigarette.

Daisy closes her eyes and inhales.

Anyhow, says Polonsky, I frame this bates but good. The kid digs the prat like a pro and out he comes with a tweezer poke but oops – here Polonsky takes a long drag on his cigarette – the poke's got one of them chains hooked onto the belt loops. Easy enough to unhook but the kid's just a punk and he panics. Rumbles the mark something awful so the bates starts to beef and the kid scrams. But he forgets to let go of the leather and he runs and runs and rips the chain right off the pants and the pants right off the goddamn leg and this bates don't know what to do standing there garters and all in the middle of the fucking street and me, I wasn't made, so I did something I've never done before or since: I talked to the mark. I said: Mister, you okay? And he says: This is so embarrassing. And I says: Oh? And he nods and points down to his shoes. Blue socks and brown oxfords.

Daisy snorts and then Mona shows up.

So, she says. What's new?

Eli does not move. Stands behind the crowd, his view of the accident blocked by the backs of tiptoed gawkers. Up and down they go, anything for a better look. He holds still one minute more, brief hesitation turning into a tilt of the head. He gets a glimpse of the Bathurst Street hill. He puts his right foot forward. Enters the crowd and steadily elbows his way up front. Face to face with a matchstick-chewing constable.

Star man, says Eli.

The constable thumbs him through.

More cops on the other side of the crowd, a good dozen of them scattered around the intersection. Stern postures that sway with the rubberneckers. On the east side of Davenport, Eli eyeballs the smashed vehicles. Guston's Bread truck dented down the middle where the police car hit, the auto's sleek lines crenellated on impact. Both drivers' doors are open and unhinged. Below, two men in white kneel beside the injured officer and lean in until their grimace-shaped spines have no further give. Shattered glass glistens all over the road and in everyone's nostrils is the smell of fresh bread.

Eli looks around. Spots a man with a bloody nose and *Guston's* stitched into his shirt, staring up at the steady gathering of cumulus. Eli walks up to him.

Morenz, from the *Star*. How's the beak?

Lotta blood, but the docs said I'll be okay.

What happened?

Shit if I know, brother. They just came roaring down the hill and smacked into me. Right fucking into me. Boom.

Boom.

Yup. Course they got the worst of it.

Was the siren on?

Yeah yeah, they were in a real hurry, you know? But they came down the hill so fast I didn't have no time. No time at all.

Wet flakes start to fall. The bread man reaches into his breast pocket for a cigarette. Small splats of blood across the Guston's logo, crimson serif of the letter S a slightly darker shade.

The bread man exhales a long line of smoke. Shit, brother, this is going to cost my boss a lot of dough.

Eli smiles.

What? What'd I say?

The wet snow comes down and down. Drops of slushy water bounce off the entablature of the Front Street portico, drip down the colonnade onto the scattered hats and heads of the scurrying. Some don't chance it. Mona stays dry. She shifts her weight from one foot to the other. On her left side, a squat dowager hefts a matronly bosom and sighs.

Sheeeee-eesh.

More people come through the doors of the station. Shove forward so small ripples of movement edge along the bodies, ripple wider until an egress grows ten feet to Mona's right. She sees Chesler impatiently elbow his way free, turn up his collar and then start across the street. More people leave the portico. Mona strikes a match and blows smoke from a mouth set tight. Whispers of nicotine loosen the jaw and leave her eager for the next drag. One after the other she inhales, until the precipitation comes to a full stop and her fingernails grow patiently yellow.

Chesler pulls his jacket over his head and runs, a hump skirting the slush. His shoes make small splashes that undulate half a foot outward before dissipating near a streetcar stop. Five men get ready to board so Chesler, with lungs burning, picks up the pace and tags on. Six of them now taking tiny steps forward, a procession slower than exhale. Chesler huffs and stares at all the hands that bulge in the kickouts. Britches that jingle. Everyone fishing for change. Another step, another. Chesler grits his teeth because a long day of two-dollar pokes gets even longer during this moment of silver. He takes one more deep breath and then stretches his fingers across a chasm of inches.

He comes home and quickly undresses. Suit and tie hit the floor, clothes that give him a sucker's anonymity. He crosses the room in an old undershirt, tweed cap pulled low on the face. With a shot of whiskey in his hand, he settles into a big-backed chair. Takes a sip, warmth and release after another day of grinding it up. Day after day after day. Commotion and gesture that coalesce into nothing but small change. He rubs his forearms, massages his palms. Wasn't turned out to be one of these nickel-and-dime schnooks. Nope. Not like her. The best stall he's ever seen and still she's happy with a couple cheap scores. Rag her about it and then she chirps the same sorry tune: *Times are tough. So what?*

For a cannon like Chesler, the slow end of the whiz comes down the muscles of his forearms, eases up at the cartilage in his fingers. The trepidatious racket gives him a tight grip on the shot glass. He knocks one back, then another.

From his desk, Eli observes the origins of copy. Watches reporters race out of the newsroom and return within the hour, possessed of answers who, what, where, when and, if possible, why. They hastily sit and start to type, cudgelling events into coherence. Some do this in total silence. Others mutter to themselves. Still more pace the floor and badger their fellows with so little restraint that the entire women's section was seated out of earshot of the four-letter words that leap out, like perverts, from the anxious newsroom.

Shit piss fuck, says Mackintosh, the City Hall man.

Eli looks over. What's up? he says.

Another protest piece.

Yeah?

Some nut says he's going to march out front of City Hall for three days straight.

What's he after?

Fair wage. Same old thing.

Three days is a long time, says Eli.

Says he's got nothing to lose. Says he's a goddamned soman … sonab … what the fuck's the word again?

Somnambulist, says Eli.

Says he walks in his fucking sleep.

Ten minutes later. A pimply boy in a peaked cap rips the pages out of Mackintosh's Underwood and runs them over to the copy desk where Johnson, ancient and hawk-nosed, takes few pains to properly place the modifiers. A snap of the fingers. Another boy grabs the edited pages and descends, one floor down, to the composing room where the type is transformed. Cast into lead. Set onto steel plates. Another descent and plates are affixed to the presses that roar tremendously and spew sheets and sheets and sheets of newsprint. The papers are cut, folded and finally delivered into the denizens' hands six times daily, seven in summer.

After loitering in the cold, Mona comes home. Upstairs, she steps into steam. Hot water stalks her ankles, thighs, then back. The minutes scald before she surrenders to temperature. She lies deep in the tub. Only her face remains above the surface, a mask of air. With every breath, concentric circles push outward from her head. Grow larger, larger, and then they vanish. She closes her eyes.

Early lessons. She watched the whiz ramble through three rooms on Cecil Street. No rhythm to what she saw. Squabble and arrest made most two-handed mobs tenuous. Her father and a succession of big-hipped, childless women who nurtured the girl with their own kind of instinct. Agnes, the thumb-wrestler, who expounded on tendon and guile. Bella. Her hugs were only skin and bones, but her perfume outweighed them all, a heavy lavender that hung in the air and briefly hid a mouldy avarice. And Francie, her favourite, who gave her cigarettes and showed her the boost. The three of them spent evenings at home. The old man silent in his chair. Mona, with a smoke in the corner of her mouth, tried to strike a match. Three bent matchsticks beside her feet.

Francie laughed.

Like this, honey. No no. This.

The careless tapping of ash. They left cigarette burns on the sofa and stolen silk camisoles hanging off the end table, the draped ghosts of past mothers.

She joined the whiz at fifteen. Tagged along to the train station and spent hours hustling the doniker for small change. Men passed by. She loitered near the men's room with her face in the newspaper. One eye out. Stared at the bone in her wrist. Adolescence concealed in her father's coat and cap, but the body inched out. Conspicuous, suddenly culpable. Gawky at five feet two.

She followed the mark inside.

Chose a stall to his right and wiped damp palms on the sides of her coat. She counted to calm herself. Forty-seven, forty-eight, forty-nine, fifty. Numbers silent in her head and then her hand started to make noise. She rolled a silver dollar along the floor, from her stall to his. The slow, rattling distraction. In three revolutions of the coin, she got a glimpse of wingtips and a big white thigh. Sparse follicle. She came out of his pants pockets with quarters and dimes and a crumpled bill. The mark cursed. He was in a shackle of dropped trou, going nowhere. But Mona was off and running out the door, in the dense station crowds. Her small hands full of change.

Mona matured in three rooms. She started in the kitchen, feeling heat off the boiler and then grifted along routes of cold tile. Past dirty glasses on the counter and stolen dishes in the sink. The old man was one step behind.

Keep moving, he said.

Breath and spittle on the lobe of her ear.

Stay on the balls of your feet.

Mucid syllables turned thick in her brain. She grew conscious of every step. Moved with dolorous precision into the sitting room. Edged around the hard angles of daylight and coffee table. Bumped into a big chair.

Careful, he said.

Toes curled in her shoes. She kept moving and moving, inched into the bedroom, stepped over a hat and into the crinkle of splayed newspaper. She looked down and saw a tie still knotted. Polka-dot pattern.

Now, he said.

She slowed down. Moved forward but leaned back. Stalled her father with a gentle nudge of elbows. The floor creaked. Tension in her calves. Stress ran the calibrations of hip, a harsh curve from her buttocks to his crotch. Her prat planted with too much strain.

No no no no, he said.

His hands grew stern. He grabbed her wrist. She blinked at the ridge of knuckles and then he let her go and she blinked at the dark outline of his fingers. His imprint on her, a dark heredity.

Do it again, he told her.

She nodded and returned to the kitchen.

Mona lifts her head out of the water. She stands up. Gooseflesh in the cool air. Water rushes off her body, dripping from her fingers into the tub with the tiniest sound.

Out of the corner of his eye, Eli watches the whispers wind around the curve of the city desk. From one editor to the next, mouths move in nearly unnatural duplication so each offers the same questioning puss. Psst-psst, they say. Psst-psst. Bert curses in the middle of the floor, nickel-cigar stub jammed into the corner of his mouth like a crooked brown tooth. Behind him is the city desk, shaped like a horseshoe but not nearly as lucky. The scene of endless diatribes, twenty-two firings and three fistfights. Mackintosh swivels in his chair, elbow garters as tight as his held tongue. Eli lowers his gaze, looks instead at the fingertips of his right hand sitting motionless on the keys HJKL. No words come from that combination of letters, not even a single syllable that can help him start his story. The lede lingers somewhere along the route of metal, skin and skull and all he can do is slouch lower in his chair and cautiously retrace that route over and over and over again.

Police car crashes into truck

Officers responding to an emergency encountered one of their own this afternoon when a police automobile hurtled down the Bathurst St. hill and collided with a bread truck on Davenport Rd. Constables Ed McGirr and Bill Pumps were racing to a holdup at the Dupont branch of the Bank of Montreal. The machine was approaching speeds of 50 miles per hour at the time of impact, which generated enough force to shatter the windshield and loosen the door on the driver's side.

Both officers received medical attention at the scene.

Fred Gallo, driver for Guston's Bread, was also under the watchful eye of a doctor after the collision. He suffered some minor cuts. He said he knew he was going to get hit, but had no chance to hit the brakes.

'They sure picked up a lot of speed down that hill. There wasn't much time to worry about my bread.'

Mona plants her prat. Chesler pinches the poke.

She sits on her bed, blanket and the front page bunched off to the side, and opens the deck of cards. Cuts them. Taps the edge of them against her open palm and watches the red lines emerge and fade in her flesh. She shuffles. The cards curve under her thumb, a pleasant resistance. Mona deals, a game of Klondike across wrinkled bedsheets. Keeps her hands busy while the mind wanders around Union. A wrong spot for weeks. And Chesler's offices, his brief clucks and exhalations, now sounding sharper in her ears. Nothing new there. For five years, she has endured his minor frustrations and kept the mob moving, day after screaming day, in the rigidly defined roles of their racket. What else is there? She glances at her options. Four of spades onto five of hearts onto six of clubs. Nothing else. She deals from the top. Ten of spades onto jack of diamonds and then nothing. Nothing, nothing, nothing, nothing. An ace on top and then the deck is done. She peeks at the face-down cards. Finds the nine of hearts and uses it. Another ace too, because she never can play this game without cheating.

Mona plants her prat. Chesler pinches the poke.

He covers a labour protest at College and Spadina. Almost at the intersection before folks are suddenly shoulder to shoulder. Feet on the march and placards held high. A gathering of the local needle trades, shmatte workers filing from the west and the south toward the grass-and-stone nexus of Queen's Park. Eli gets pushed toward a presser named Nodelman.

We want someone who is with us square!

Uh.

Not these gonifs what all they do is take and take!

Okay, says Eli.

Nodelman gesticulates with his index finger. His mouth opens but his next words are lost to labour's growing discord. Voices Yiddish and Ukrainian squish together in the sparse wiggle room of protest, a polyglot glut of tongues that needs nearly a whole minute to ease into harmony.

FAIR WAGE!

FAIR WAGE!

FAIR WAGE!

FAIR WHHH-eeeeeeeeeeeeeeeeeeeeeeeeeee!

First come the police whistles and then the quartet of cops who jump down the front steps of the station. Others follow. Push and shove, push and shove. Eli gets grabbed by the collar and spun around.

Star man, says Eli. *Star* man!

What're you doing here?

Trying to get a story.

The officer draws his truncheon, knuckles going white at the ridge. Well, he says, get it and go.

Again, Eli files his story fitfully. Then heads home, where he slouches in his armchair with the funnies open in his lap. After a week of newspaper ruckus, he has trouble settling into his own silences. He shifts his weight. Through his tiny apartment window, the setting sun leaves a scar of light across his neck and chest and legs.

The tip's monotonous division of labour leaves Mona no less attentive. Crammed in among the frantic waves and aborted runs of the arrivals concourse, she nonetheless fronts with such gorgeous acuity that Chesler is almost a half-second too slow on the fan. But he locates. Offices for her to come through. She reverses position on the mark, a hunched Hasid burdened with two bulging suitcases, and doubles back toward Chesler. She knows the way the moment has stretched so ungainly that Chesler has been unable to score the pit. Office for a second frame rumbles in her ear and she shadows the Hasid up the stairs.

In the Great Hall, a couple kisses farewell. Others bunch obliviously near the departure ramp. Mona wanders compliantly, all elbows, while she watches the back of the Hasid's head. His yarmulke askew like a large lazy eye. Chesler clucks. Dawdlers begin to thicken around the announcement boards and Mona sets a new frame. Hips planted, buttocks sway with such discreet allure the Hasid almost ossifies. Chesler makes his move. His hands an argosy of want.

They cut up the scores in a talkie. Slouched in the darkness of the Alhambra Theatre, mumbling Chesler cusses the paucity of every poke he cleans out. Shush go the audience members on either side of him, shush. Mona beside him watches the picture, a Durante and Keaton comedy whose recent sense of sound is at odds with the flickering speed of images. Mugs of beer shatter flatly on the screen. Jokes hiss. An actor trips and slaps the ground long after he could be back up. Mona chuckles nonetheless. Elbows Chesler. Chesler mumbles. SHUSH! He rifles the fat poke of the Hasid, eager fingers finding nothing but black-and-white photos of frowsy nude women. No bills. In the shimmering light of the movie screen, he gets an eyeful. Pose after pose of cunt and tit. He opens his mouth; nothing comes out for the first second and then he says, HOL-eee –

SHUSH!

Queen's Park protest turns violent

Toronto's needle workers are bloodied but unbowed after yesterday's protest was transformed from a peaceful demonstration into a struggle between police and labour.

Members of the Industrial Union of Needle Trade Workers began to gather at Queen's Park just after noon. A smattering of workers quickly grew into a dense crowd, many of them with a common chant of 'Fair wage.' The mass of people swelled toward the south end of the provincial seat of government before the local constabulary arrived on foot.

They were soon accompanied by members of Chief Draper's mounted 'Red Squad.'

Words between police and the demonstrators heated up quickly, with pushing and shoving making matters worse. The chant from the crowd of workers grew louder when the mounted police arrived.

'All we want is a fair wage,' said Efrim Nodelman, a pants presser from T. Eaton Co. 'We don't want any trouble. We just want to say our piece.'

The police arrested several protesters. Myron Kleig, Sid Goodis and Lou Markfield, all of the Pacific Pants Ltd., were charged with sedition and creating a public disturbance.

From the kitchen table she turns, holding a bottle in each hand. Daisy takes two quick steps into the living room, then slows. Faint bustle comes from the corner table, where Slotsky leans close to his girl. Daisy passes by and hears a joke half-told, the creaking of chairs. She keeps going, the bottles growing heavy in her arthritic hands.

Fuck, she says.

A stutter step toward the middle, where Levitz and Lippman chop it up. She places one of the bottles on the table.

Thanks, Daisy.

Sure.

Join us. Take a load off.

Later.

She keeps weaving, a near-sober sequence between Hashmall, who used to front for Benny the Yid, and a street-corner Bolshevik named Rossen, who slurs words from his rehearsed speeches to anyone who passes by. Daisy has heard it all before. She angles away from him but then jostles another customer so hard a whiskey jumps the rim of a glass.

Hey!

Sorry.

With a deep breath, she stops at her usual table, where Mona reads the racing form to Polonsky, and Chesler, red-eyed and appetent, holds out his glass.

Daisy pours.

Thanks, says Chesler.

Sure.

Chesler looks into his glass. Looks up. Elbows Mona.

Uh-huh, says Mona.

It's been three weeks now, says Chesler. Maybe more.

Three weeks of what?

Of this nickel-and-dime stuff. Putting in my day and getting nothing back but dribs and drabs.

Times're tough.

Yeah yeah.

They knock one back. Chesler runs his forefinger around the rim of his glass. He's halfway to stinko.

Maybe it won't get no better, he says.

Mona looks up from the racing form. You say that every time we hit a rough patch, she says.

Yeah yeah yeah.

Things go late. Chesler still full of ginger at half past three, so he steps outside where the air is cool like whispers and the moon waxes across an empty stretch of Spadina. He looks to his left and walks out of the alley. The quiet street slips away from him, steals down parallel lines so the dark pavement meets the night sky in deceitful new horizons.

He follows. Through a lonely intersection, then long blocks where brick and shadow fuse with lugubrious affinity. He sees locked doors drain away, a keystone go dim. Fragments of buildings float beyond eye level and connect near the corner where a street lamp burns.

Chesler stops.

Smiles.

Coins come out of his pocket and he aims for the loose yellow circle of lamplight. Flat clank of a penny on glass. He flings copper harder and harder until he hears a crash like laughter. More laughter at the words in his head. *Small-timer. Public drunkenness. Van*-CRASH-*dal*-CRASH-*ism*!

Well into the night when Mona shoves the cards aside. Countless games of Klondike no match for her restless fingers. She straightens up in the bed. Yawns. Arched shoulders and tired arms stretch, loosen. Ten fingers interlock and slowly pull apart. The gentle pronouncements of cartilage. Beside her, a candle flickers by the window. Three other walls mumbling; down the hall, Polonsky talks in his sleep. His voice, garbled and wrought, escapes his room and lingers in the house like hangover.

Mona yawns again. Runs a hand across the length of her cheek, slows slightly where knuckle meets jawbone and continues down her throat. With only the tips of fingers, she crosses over the ridge of breastbone and then the faintest brush of aureole. She inhales. A single finger now, skulking between the legs with practiced delicacy. Lubricious digit that closes the gap between touch and feel so her back presses deep into the pillows and candlelight smears the shadows that fall, like hair, over her face.

She comes.

Almost a month back at the paper and none of his copy comes close to page one. He covers awning fires and visits settlement houses, small-time stuff that writes itself and leaves lots of time for foot-dangling. Eli eyeballs his scuffed brogans, evidence of all the recent legwork. Stepping slowly back into the game, he is using the easy give-and-take of interviews to feel his way forward. Get comfortable with words again. As a rookie, he simply mimicked the sardonic patter of the veteran press boys. Now, amidst laces and tongue, he mulls a more certain locution.

Look alive, Morenz.

He looks up and Bert jams an address into his hand.

Eli stands on the sidelines of the police training field and watches a muster of very large men fall into formation. Series of lines arranged by instrument. Flutes and piccolos are readied, rope drums slung over big shoulders. Hammers of the glockenspiel are held tight just as Jones, the short, bespectacled director of the Police Fife and Drum Band, clears his throat and shoves a finger into the warm spring air.

The drum major takes his cue and beats off. Dum-ba dum-ba dum-ba dum-ba. His bandmates follow with a rigorous bam and blow that mangles the opening bars of 'God Save the King.'

Stop, says Jones. Stop! Stop!

The band stops.

Jones points to a tall piccoloist in the back row.

You. McMaster. Blow.

McMaster takes a deep breath. His chest rises and falls in slow, distinct stages. He lifts his instrument, a vein in the neck goes tense and resplendent. Bulbous cheeks shove out note after shrill note.

Stop, says Jones. Stop! Stop!

McMaster stops.

Jones shakes his head. Six tone holes, he says. Only six. Think you can get it right?

McMaster blinks. Looks at the piccolo, so slender in his meaty hands.

Jones thumbs him to the sidelines.

Practice, McMaster. Practice practice practice.

But.

Go over there and suck that pickle.

But.

Suck it!

Eli watches McMaster walk his way. Square jaw lowered, shoulders braced like scaffold.

Rough, says Eli. Rough to be singled out like that.

Shit, says McMaster. I wasn't so bad, was I?

I don't know anything about music.

No worse than any of them other guys. Gleason? Flanders? Yost? We all sound the same.

I don't know.

I do. It's a cinch. And none of them better give me any lip about it, neither.

Hope not.

The large man looks closely at Eli. Ain't seen you before, he says. Where're you from? Bunco?

The *Star*.

Oh shit. Are you going to put this in the paper?

Don't worry, says Eli. We'll call this background.

Yeah?

Yeah.

That's good. I don't want any trouble.

You won't get any from me. I'm Morenz.

McMaster.

They shake hands. Eli asks more questions. The answers obfuscated by the swelling discord of 'Vimy Ridge,' which follows the band as they march round and round, leaving a soaring crescendo in the air and size-fourteen indentations in the grass.

Police play a different tune

Toronto officers who regularly devote their time to more serious matters will have the chance to enjoy some lighter fare tomorrow afternoon when the Police Fife and Drum Band kicks off the city centenary celebrations.

The event will begin at 10:30 in the morning outside Union Station and proceed up University Avenue to City Hall. The band will perform inspirational favourites such as 'Vimy Ridge' and 'Marche Lorraine.'

'We have a very musical force,' said Purvis Jones, director of the band. 'I'll wager we have one of the top bands in the Dominion.'

The 37-member band is made up of officers from all divisions. Director Jones said regular rehearsal schedules are often disrupted because many of his musicians get called to duty. 'I lost half my flute section to a bank job last week,' he said.

Jones added that many of the men have been practicing around their regular shifts to ensure that they will all be ready when the city celebrates its birthday tomorrow. 'I guarantee it will be a fine show.'

Chesler slaps the paper down on the tabletop. FWAP! Whiskey rattles in three glasses. See, he says. This is just what we've been waiting for.

Mona and Daisy peer down at the article. Polonsky sits still.

Are you nuts? says Mona. There'll be more cops there than at HQ.

It'll be a push grift, says Chesler. A real push grift.

Yeah but.

And these're the well-heeled we're talking about. Them pokes'll be fat.

I don't know about this, says Mona.

Why not?

What's wrong with our regular spot?

What's wrong? Fuck. We've been pissing nickels for months now. I can't stand it anymore. You think we can just wait and wait and something good will come along, but no way, sister. Nothing doing.

Mona sips her drink. Returns the glass quietly to the table.

Polonsky lights a cigarette. You know, he says, I worked this parade once. Back in '27, I think. There was plenty to go around. Lot of coppers there, but they weren't no different from anyone else. Ride a big fat bundle on their hips as easy as it was hidden in the seams. And they don't savvy none either. Unless you're talking whiz copper – then it's another thing entirely. That's one poke you don't want to pinch.

Daisy reaches for Polonsky's smoke. She takes a deep drag. This ain't '27, baby. Times've changed.

I know I know. I'm just saying is all.

Chesler turns to Mona. So what do you say?

Mona shrugs. Looks at Polonsky.

Listen, honey, Polonsky says. You got to work where you feel it's a right spot. But this sounds like a regular tip, more or less. Lot of suckers.

Lot of suckers, says Chesler.

As long as you got the moxie, says Polonsky.

Chesler folds his arms. Course.

A warm spring sun droops onto the backs of the Fife and Drum Band. They sweat in full ceremonial regalia and spread out at arm's length. Bubbles of nervous laughter flatten into a strict silence for one second, two, three. Then bum-ba bum-ba bumba goes the drum major. Bum-ba bum-ba replies the rest of the percussion section, followed by the first notes of the wind instruments. Soon 'Vimy Ridge' is in full swing. The band begins to march, moving from the Dominion Public Building, along the Front Street extension and up the westward slant of University Avenue. Pop pop pop go the flashbulbs. In the portion of a second needed for the shutter to open and close, marchers hastily slow into absolute stillness, poses that will linger into the next edition of the papers. Pop pop, they are illuminated. Deep lines in their faces, a fold in the clothes. Pop. Abbott, the photographer, pauses to change a bulb. Beside him, Eli describes the scene. He writes *rousing music* and *packed avenue*. He writes *failed stretch of sidewalk*. In less penurious times, the city had planned for mass construction all the way up the street. The new building of the Parker Fountain Pen Company screamed progress via the perpetual assemblage of nibs. The neon weather beacon atop the Canada Life Building forecast continued prosperity. Back then, Eli quoted an endless parade of black-tie types who boasted of all the expected ribbon cuttings. Then the slump deepened and the hoopla became barely sibilant. Construction stopped. Skeletal forms stood empty and unfinished, so even now, less than three years later, Eli still sees a combination of growth and depression every step of the way.

A long narrow triangle of napes. This is what Chesler sees. Cloche hats and fedoras that advance up the street. Banners above gently ripple the words *Toronto 1834 to 1934*. From the back end of the line, he has his choice of fat marks, well-dressed men carrying the evidence of three squares above their belts. This crowd is a real kick in the pants. Six scores in and Chesler can locate by sight. Through the crook of an elbow he catches a left britch impression big enough for a blind man to spot. He restrains a smile, recklessly tossing away seconds now that there seems to be an eternity in the coffers. He shuffles his feet. Offices for a frame.

Everybody begins to inch forward. Contour of the crowd shifts with each step. An elbow juts out of nowhere, profiles bunch and separate. Within this brief rearrangement, Eli spots two familiar faces and hustles after them. Judge Tinker and an attorney named Snodgrass. Two men, eminently quotable, whose frequent appearances in the press belie an ability to construct a full sentence.

These celebrations, you know, says the judge. How important.

Snodgrass nods and nods. Exactly what I was.

Really a showcase.

Spectacle that.

The type of event that can bring our city a little.

A lot.

Yes, a lot of it.

Eli takes notes. They move further up the line, almost near City Hall, when Abbott appears, camera at the ready.

Okay. One picture of all of you.

Pop pop.

Mona turns from the flash. Too late. She has given up her kisser to the camera, her face captured on film. With a quick intake of breath she steps back and to the left, while the crowd continues to plod past her. This tiny change of pace not nearly enough because she should run run run from this spot, but out of the chatter and enjambment comes another office from Chesler. Set the frame. So she does. Eases back into the tip and finds the mark and his friends moving up the line. Phrases like *civic pride* and *good clean fun* float back her way, but the only word in her ears is *frame*. Set the frame, stay out of the camera frame. Mona shifts her weight, stays poised on the balls of her feet so her sudden homonymy won't crumb the play. She takes a step, sets her heels. Plants her prat.

Three seconds before the music stops, Eli suddenly flinches, a feeling small and substantial as a pore of skin. He looks around. Cheekbones and sideburns cram his vision. Nothing out of the ordinary, so with a shrug he finesses his way to the cenotaph, where Abbott, Tinker and Snodgrass applaud. Cheers and whistles and hoo-haws. Eli makes notes while Abbott aims and fires. Pop pop. Tinker keeps clapping, Snodgrass jams his hands in his pockets and looks around furiously and the applause continues even as Mayor Stewart appears at the podium and says, My fellow Torontonians.

Part Two

April 1934

Eli pushes a red tray along a metal track. Slowly, past biscuits and a basket of apples gone yellow. Plates and plates of indistinguishable sandwiches. The special at the Bowles Lunch is alphabet soup. Behind the counter, a fat woman with a pencil behind her ear stirs the pot. Eli gets coffee.

He sits by the window. Sun and cloud fight for space on the other side of the glass. He takes a sip. Over the rim of his mug comes Bert Murneau. Puffing on a cigar. Soup and milk slosh onto his tray. He pulls up a chair.

Morenz.

Bert.

Bert gulps his milk. His Adam's apple bounces. Good job on that celebration business.

Eli nods.

What're your plans now?

I was thinking of getting some biscuits.

After that.

Eli shrugs.

No plans?

Nope.

Bert finishes his milk and wipes his mouth with the back of his hand. Still some white on the lips. His cigar has gone out.

Heading home then.

I guess so.

Bert twirls his spoon in the soup. Letters churn in the broth. An *M* flips over to become a *W*.

Easing yourself back in. That's good, Morenz, that's very good. You'll need your rest.

Oh?

I'd like you to keep working this pickpocket angle.

Pickpockets? I'm a city man. What do I know about crime?

What's to know? There's good guys and there's bad guys.

But, says Eli.

I think you're ready to handle this. Now don't get me wrong. I'm not trying to push, but you've always known your way around the old notepad. And we need a man on this. You're that man, Morenz. And as long as you can tell me you're on the ball – Bert taps his temple – up here, it's a done deal.

Bert finishes his soup and relights his cigar. Leans back, puffing. Enormous minutes of silence.

Okay, says Eli.

The front door of the house opens and an oblong light leaks down two stairs. She comes out. Brimless blue hat, jacket in a darker shade. Pulls the handle and the door wedges into the frame, the lock turns with a sound like teeth grinding.

Out of the alley she walks, slowly, stopping only a moment when a surprisingly warm breeze blows through thin budding maples. Mona holds on to her hat and heads south on Spadina, west on Dundas. Into Kensington Market she goes, whistling a tune that gets tangled in the dull click of her own heels.

She reaches for an apple. Inspects it. Turns it coolly over, red skin and fingernails at every angle. She curls her lip. Other hands slip past, fat elbows collide. Bushels of women in the market this afternoon. They move down the aisles in strange unison, feeling fruit. Wire baskets slung over forearms. Mona palms the apple and wanders down the bins. Plums and apricots hide in the pockets of her coat. She looks for space. Across the floor, a woman tsk-tsks a bruised pear. Mona stops. Her hand lingers over the celery, stalks like long useless fingers.

Munching an apple along the clank and rustle of Kensington shops. Past moisture-covered windows and the open door of a dry goods, where two old women spit on their hands and pull out wooden stalls. A cobbler adjusts his awning for the flap of words.

SHOE SHINE 5c. HATS BLOCKED. Mona takes three bites more and tosses the core into a trash bin. Hand in her pocket draws a cigarette from a crumpled pack. She feels in the lining for a matchstick in front of the butcher's window, where plucked chickens hang and a man chews loudly on a cigar. Dots of blood on his sleeve and forearm.

Light? he asks.

Mona holds the unlit cigarette between two fingers and nods.

Back on Spadina, Mona stops at a newsstand. Browses the glossies and pulps, picking through *Ballyhoo* and *Real Detective*. Smiles at the lurid colour of *Screenbook*, the endless promises to astound and reveal. She balances the spine of the magazine in her palm and uses the big, floppy pages to shade her duke. With a deft movement of wrist and fingers, she stashes away two candy bars. Keeps one eye askance for the vendor, who taps his foot slowly, almost imperceptibly, at the opposite end of the row. Mona is wary of the impatient beat. She replaces the magazine and appeases him with two pennies for the newspaper. Crosses the street before she is halted by the headline. Small story on the bottom of the page that leaves her stiff, like a new deck of cards.

Angry judge complains about 'sticky-fingered desperados'

One of Toronto's most prominent legal minds lashed out at a 'sickness' on our city streets yesterday.

'This pickpocket business is getting pretty bad,' said Judge Orland Tinker of the municipal court. 'People should feel free to wander anywhere in our city without fear of losing their wallet to these sticky-fingered desperados.'

Bank robbers get more notice because of their violent methods and large sums of cash, but it is the cowardly pickpocket who now requires swift attention, said the judge. 'It's a sickness on its way to a plague.'

Judge Tinker said he felt compelled to speak out after last week's city centenary celebrations, during which several ordinary citizens were robbed under the noses of the city's top officers. The team of pickpockets, dubbed the Centenary Mob, is still at large.

It's small potatoes, Morenz.

I know.

Couple cheap grifters hit it big for once in their lives and suddenly you fellows are all over it.

I know, says Eli again.

McMaster keeps walking his beat. Gives a sideways glance now and then. Eyes and feet apace, past a crack in the sidewalk and City Hall and cigarette butts dropped and crushed. Diners and pawn shops and furriers, an easy accumulation of city blocks in his long stride. Eli, half a foot shorter, hustles to keep up.

I just need some background, says Eli.

McMaster shrugs.

A place to start.

McMaster pauses across from the Colonial Theatre and silently mouths a few words off the marquee.

So?

Listen, Morenz. The whiz is the lowest racket there is. Believe me. Anything out of their mouths is just a bunch of chewing gum.

Eli smiles. The wind kicks up. Litter scatters from his feet.

Shit, says McMaster. Try Little Freddie. He might talk.

Where do I find him?

Mona heads home. Finds Daisy, alone in the living room, with her feet up on a tattered divan. Smoking. Beside her, a radio plays low and full of static so the sounds of Bert Niosi are only garbled hum.

Just missed Ida Keyes, says Daisy.

Who?

Ida Keyes. Rip-and-tear girl. We did a little time together. She was here with Dago Joe. I think they monkey around.

Mona shrugs.

You know Joe. Big mouth. Gap teeth.

Hmm, says Mona. Seen Chesler?

Nope.

Seen the paper?

Daisy leans forward. Swings her feet to the floor.

They're kicking up a fuss over that touch we pulled.

Don't start fretting, honey. News today and trash tomorrow.

Maybe.

Maybe nothing.

But.

Listen, says Daisy, if you're gonna keep yapping, do it over lunch. I'm starved.

Tap room of the Lansdowne Hotel. In the dim light, Eli finds his way across the floor, each table he passes a warren of plot and malice. Flat-nosed men jaw with rouged women. Bark of laughter behind him, but he stares straight ahead. Sees the barman, six and a half feet tall, flip open a newspaper. Eli walks over, rests a foot on the trestle.

Little Freddie?

The barman looks up from the funnies. A bony finger marks his place on the second panel of *Wash Tubbs*.

Yup.

Morenz, from the *Star*.

So?

I'm doing a piece on the whiz. Maybe you can help.

Freddie reaches across the bar with his long left arm and drags a glass back. Draws a draught.

Maybe, he says.

Eli looks at his beer. Takes a sip.

What do you think about this pickpocket business at City Hall?

Freddie shrugs. Well-heeled bunch, he says. Push grift.

A what?

Push grift, says Freddie. A slow-moving tip. Dense crowd. Rip-and-tear mobs love it. Rumble all they want and no one'll beef gun.

Beef gun?

Call the cops.

Oh.

Bang-up operators could care less. Find action in a phone booth.

Eli takes a swig of beer.

So what're you saying?

Freddie looks side to side, leans all the way across the bar so he and Eli are nose to nose.

I'm saying it was small-timers. I'm saying Jew mob.

Oh.

That's the word. Normally that info'd cost. But I hate the mockies.

Uh-huh.

Still owe me for the beer, though.

Eli tosses some coins on the bar and walks away.

In the grandstand of the Dufferin Race Track, hundreds of people shift to get a good look. The ponies make the turn and the announcer's nasal crackle prods all ears peripatetic, mad, and the money keeps moving from hand to hand. Chesler takes the side bet from Slotsky and shakes his monied fist down toward the track.

Yes yes yes yes yes.

Slotsky slaps Chesler's back and points at the onrushing horse.

No, says Chesler. No no no no no no.

... and out of the pack it's Gooseberry followed by Cahoots, Vigorish aaaaannd Two Bits, Gooseberry going strong, Cahoots and Vigorish picking it up, Vigorish moving up on the inside now, neck and neck with Cahoots, followed by Two Bits, and it's Gooseberry still out front with Vigorish, Cahoots aaaaaaaaannnd Two Bits, Gooseberry pulling out front with Vigorish rounding the corner, Gooseberry and Vigorish, Gooseberry, Vigorish, Gooseberry into the home stretch, it'll be close, folks, real close, Gooseberry Vigorish Gooseberry Vigorish Gooseberrr-eeeee and it's Vigorish by a nose ...

Fuck, says Chesler.

In the last booth of Eisner's, Eli gathers more dope. He writes and nods, writes and nods, while Itch Goldfarb hunches over the table and lights one cigarette after another. Blows all kinds of smoke.

Listen. Any mob in town could've pulled off this baby. Easy. A tip like that. Could use a gimp for a cannon and still get plenty of kick.

Itch sips his beer.

Tell you one thing, though. The stall was a good one. Put that in your paper. Folks always say the cannon makes the touch 'cause he's the one who forks the leather, but don't believe that for a second. No sir. The stall's the one who does the heavy lifting. I should know. I stalled for thirty years and the guts of the job was always in the frame.

Why?

Nine times out of ten you're working with your back to the mark. The cannon's got the whole play right in front of him but you got to feel your way around. It takes real grift sense to do that. And it's all perfectly natural, see? You don't do nothing to draw attention to yourself. Just set the frame nice and easy and then hold it there until the cannon can get his duke down.

You mean put his hand in the pocket?

Naw, not the whole hand. Just the tips of two fingers. But that's my point. Any joe just turned out can make the dip, but it's a rare breed that can throw up his hump. That's why a good stall stays a stall. Always in demand. Take me, for example. I was a pretty sharp prat digger in my day. Could work a tog. Bang a souper. But as far as the mobs in this town were concerned, I was a stall and nothing more.

Itch strikes a match. In the brief spasm of firelight, Eli can see the older man's unkempt eyebrows. Dilated pupils.

What was your name again? says Itch.

Morenz.

Right. Morenz. That's why I blew, Morenz. Couldn't call my own shots. This was '27 maybe. Or '28. Before the slump anyway, and I knew there'd be lots of work out there so I muzzled around the 'Peg for a while. St. Paul. Spent four months in Minny and pinched the biggest poke of my life. Federal building on Hennepin. This big old bates going through a revolving door and I'm right there with him. True story! Ask anyone!

Sure, says Eli.

Mona and Daisy argue in the Automat just after noon. Hushed tones but loud hands. Fingers point, the table gets slapped.

But, says Mona.

Daisy makes a stop sign with her palm.

No buts, honey. You know the score. Chesler's earned his dough. He can do what he wants.

He wants to blow it.

So? You and him ain't doing too well, are you?

Mona stands up and walks over to the food dispenser. She jams two coins into the slot and pulls out a piece of hot apple pie. Sits back down. Stabs at the pie with her fork.

Same old story, says Daisy. Working the whiz is one thing. But having to futz around with your partner takes real moxie. Every cannon I know can't stand being off the whiz. They say they like the dough, but really all they want is action.

Mona takes a bite. Chews this one over.

Ever work off the whiz?

Sure, says Daisy. But that was always worse. There's plenty of grifters in this world, but they ain't gonna be savvy to people like us. Stick with your own kind.

My own kind drives me nuts.

You know what I always say, honey: the other rackets are plain trouble. Remember that sap man you hooked up with? What was his name?

Markson.

Right, Markson. What a bozo. And that goyish card player?

Robison.

Geez, honey, see what I'm saying? Stick with the whiz. You can't beat a man with good hands.

Daisy slices off some pie crust. A green fluorescent light blinks behind her.

After Itch runs his mouth for hours, Eli follows on foot. For the next three nights, he hobnobs in the Jewish joints that spread out from the wide intersection of Spadina and College. In delicatessens like Litvak's and the Eppes Essen, he asks questions between mouthfuls of onion bun. Answers often shrugged or murmured in an old phlegmy language. He plays games of nine ball at Libastyik's and, one night later, in Kanarick's on Brunswick, where he's quickly down five bucks to a natty grifter named Cobourg Henry.

Oh sure, I know Itch. Me, him and Solly Cling used to work three-handed down at the track. Poor schmuck.

What do you mean?

Henry chalks his cue. Heavy on the pomade, his starkly parted hair leaves a deep white line of scalp.

Itch's been off the whiz for years. No one even talks to him since he came back to town.

Why?

Henry leans, meticulous and angular, over the green felt. One eye wide. With one sure stroke, he pots a ball off the break.

Why? Eli says again.

One thing about the whiz, Morenz, is it's a very tense place to work. And you have to find a way to work off that tension.

Henry looks over the table. A wide spread. He shrugs and banks a shot off the cushion. Eli shakes his head.

Me, I shoot pool. Itch turned to junk. Happens all the time. But when it happens, you've got trouble. Because the dumb yutz on the needle is thinking about one thing only. Not the wallet. Not the sucker. The needle. It makes him irresponsible, buggy.

Henry runs the next four before getting tied up in the corner. Eli lines up his shot. The ball kisses the cushion but little else.

After a while, no one'd work with Itch. He had to leave town.

He told me he wanted to call his own shots.

Geez, Morenz, shouldn't a man in your profession know how to see through the hoo-haw?

Henry slams the next two balls home. The last one sinks in silence.

That's another fin you owe me.

Yeah, says Eli.

Now, you know who could tell you some stories?

Toronto a haven for pickpockets

Toronto the Good is a very bad place for citizens and their wallets, according to members of the underworld. In a series of exclusive and wide-ranging interviews with the Star, several thieves, under the promise of strict anonymity, said Toronto's low crime rate is actually an advantage to pickpockets, who prey on the unsuspecting.

'This goody-goody stuff is really a boon to us fellows,' said one member of the lowly profession. 'I've worked in rougher places like Winnipeg and St. Paul and, if you ask me,

their reputation makes it tougher to make a go of it. People are more alert there.'

Groups of pickpockets, known in crime circles as 'whiz' mobs, work in crowded areas such as sporting events and train stations and can steal a billfold in under ten seconds.

'That business with the Centenary Mob is a good example,' said another source, referring to the high incidence of stolen wallets at City Hall during the city centenary last month. 'That was a dense, unsuspecting crowd. We call that a "push grift" because even if you get careless and push a little too much, you can still get away with the money.'

Daisy and Mona join Polonsky during a late-afternoon lull at their place. A bottle and three glasses between them.

So it's been a few days? says Daisy.

Yup.

And no hassles? No one's been pinched?

No, says Mona.

Daisy lays a hand on Mona, gently, just above the elbow.

See? she says. It's all blown over.

Mona shrugs. Sips. Whiskey bites the tongue.

Yeah, says Polonsky. Keep fussing over this stuff and you never know what'll happen. Remember Squinty Dunkleman?

Who?

Before your time, says Daisy.

Who was he?

The Squint was a prat digger, says Polonsky. Glass eye but a real pro. Had the longest fingers you ever saw.

I'll say! says Daisy.

Polonsky grins. Refills the glasses. Silence in the room save for the bloop bloop of whiskey.

He had a little thing for Daisy. Never made a big show of it or anything, but just watching her walk into the room would rankle the poor schnook. After me and her hooked up, he really went buggy. Comes looking for me. We was working the King Eddy and I'm about to prat this bates in when the Squint shows up, pops out that glass peeper of his and starts hollering: I've got my eye on you, Polonsky! I've got my eye on you!

Polonsky laughs. Daisy drinks. Mona shakes her head and then sees him standing there.

That's a good story, says Eli.

Polonsky turns around. Who're you?

Morenz, from the *Star*.

Yeah?

Been doing a series on the whiz.

Yeah?

Don't you read the papers?

Shit, says Polonsky. Don't read at all.

Oh, says Eli. How about you ladies?

Sorry, says Daisy.

Eli looks at Mona. Olive skin, hair dark as printer's ink. She takes a sip from her glass even though there is nothing left to drink. She looks up at him and he continues to stare at her. A tunnel of pupils.

No, she says.

You sure?

Sure I'm sure.

I don't want any trouble, you know. Just want to talk.

Got nothing to say.

Even if it's confidential?

Mona shakes her head.

Eli stands still another moment. Looks around the room. Well, he says. Thanks anyway.

Sure, says Daisy.

Okay.

Eli walks out. Mona searches for a smoke.

Later. She sits on her bed with the five of clubs in hand. Slow gander and she places the card atop the six of hearts. Turns over the next one and taps it against her thigh.

Tap.

Tap.

Tap.

Tap.

Nowhere to go. Nothing to do, so she puts the card down. Drops the rest of the deck and finds a loose cigarette on the nightstand. Strikes a match. The small flame fidgets in front of her. She lights up and leans back on the bed. Blows smoke rings, grey circles asymmetrical. She closes her eyes while smoke in the shape of her mouth rises above the room.

And later. A fly, wayward and furious, buzzes around the room. Eli leans back in his chair, swivels slightly to the left and stares at the ceiling. He follows each turn of the wings, each twist, and then rolls up his newspaper. Stands. Swings.

Damn.

Bzzzz.

Damn.

Bzzzzzzzz.

His cheeks dot pink. His arm stays cocked. The fly wanders indecisively from the light fixture to the window and back before Eli stands on his chair for a better look. Nothing moves up there. Nothing makes a sound.

A big night at Daisy's. Levitz and Lippman are bending elbows. Slotsky, with an arm around his girl, grins across the table at Chesler.

Hunches, says Slotsky. That's what I'm talking about. I'm talking about playing the hunches because sometimes you just know what's what. And you know you know – you just don't know why you know. That's the kicker. It just hits you. It's like a, like …

A feeling, says his girl.

Exactly. Exactly. Like a goddamned feeling. And, honey, you can take this feeling to the bank. Even though every goddamned book in town is saying otherwise. Cahoots, they all said. Cahoots is a lock. But not me. Nope. I had my eye on this little cherry no one ever noticed.

Chesler knocks one back.

And the book on this one! Hol-eee! Odds as long as your arm. No one and I mean no one saw this coming.

Except you, says Slotsky's girl.

Except me.

Another round arrives. Chesler downs the shot and takes a long swig of beer. Slotsky slides his hand to his girl's knee. Fat fingers squeeze and wend up the thigh. Palm pressing hard. Pleasure hangs off his face like a fat necktie.

I've got a good feeling about this, too, baby.

I'll bet, says his girl.

Mona leaves her room. The faint click of the lock is loud in the empty hall. She listens to the tread of her shoes down the stairs, the soft scrape of her hand on the banister. Her descent continues through mangled laughter and music that rises up from the living room. At the foot of the stairs, she stops. Takes a swallow of air and peeks her head through the door.

Slotsky and Lippman lean awkwardly against each other. Crooning along with the radio up high.

> *I can't help it*
> *If that doggoned moon above*
> *Makes me need*
> *Someone like you to love.*

Mona moves along the edge of the chatter, angling her way silently to the table where Levitz has nodded off and Slotsky's girl snaps her fingers tunelessly. Mona does not sit down.

Where've you been? she says.

Chesler slides a nickel along the tabletop. Bounces the coin off a full ashtray and then off empty bottles shoved together like a tiny transparent skyline.

Around, he says.

It's been three days.

We're riding the cushions, doll. What's the problem?

Some reporter's been sniffing around.

Here?

Yeah.

Fuck. Did he recognize you?

Mona does not answer.

Did he recognize you? Chesler says again.

No, says Mona. No, I don't think so.

Okay.

Says he wants to write about the whiz. Learn the ins and outs.

So? says Chesler.

So maybe we should suss him out.

And give him the chance to finger you? No way.

I think we should. Just to see if he'll beef.

Fuck. Ain't you listening?

But, says Mona.

No, I said. No!

Mona stares. Shrugs. Walks away.

Back in the sonorous clacking of keys, Eli rests chin in hand. Opens his notebook. Eyeballs the script, the loop and slant of graphite that offers only faint connection to his story. An image that lurks at the edges of anecdote. The dark hair, crow's feet at the corner of her eyes. Eli rubs his chin, looks to his right where Mackintosh, in a flurry of rolled sleeves, pounds out his copy.

NOW!

A copy boy hustles up to the desk. Snatches the page then turns, taking five fast steps before he smacks into another boy rushing the opposite way. Eli watches the scene. Sheets of loose paper pummel his eyes.

The arrow on the floor indicator retreats, 6 5 4 3 2 G, and the elevator doors rumble open. A tight rectangle of people slants into a rhombus on the marble floor of the *Star* lobby. Eli frees himself from the crowd and, with hat pulled low, pushes through the front door of the building. Makes his way up Bay Street. Past office buildings like Trust and Guarantee and then the Permanent, whose bronze doors steadily emit employees at quitting time. Bookkeepers and secretaries fill the sidewalk, late editions stuffed under their arms.

At the City Hall loop, Eli jumps a short. No room to sit so he hangs on to a strap. Wobbles side to side as the streetcar begins to move. He closes his eyes for minute, opens them and sees the man across from him reading the latest whiz article. The shape of his own copy in another's mouth.

Shadow of his waist and legs stretches the length of the hallway. Turns toward the last door on the right. Hand in the left pants pocket fumbles for the keys. Nothing there. Then the right pants pocket, inside his coat. Nothing there either.

Oh-oh, says Eli.

And then he hears the jingle at the end of the hall. Jingle jingle. He turns his head. Mona walks his way, twirling the key ring on her forefinger. She stops at the opposite end of the door frame. Stares.

Tailed me from the paper, says Eli.

Uh-huh.

She hands him his wallet.

This is yours too.

Eli looks at the leather in his hand. Checks the billfold.

It's all there, says Mona. Just wanted to see if your story checks out.

And?

Mona shrugs. So far, she says.

Eli nods. Holds her in his eyes, working the retina along her mouth and jaw. Line of the neck and the hint of clavicle.

I saw you there, he says. At City Hall.

Mona shrugs again. Maybe, she says. But it's your word against mine.

Got more than words.

What?

I said I've got more than words.

What does that mean?

Meet me here, he says. Tomorrow.

I told you, says Chesler. I told you to stay away!

Smoke spirals out the corner of Mona's mouth.

Now this snoop's got you in his sights!

Polonsky rolls a cigarette. Don't go buggy just yet, he says. Let's see what his angle is first.

Sure, says Chesler. See him. But don't say nothing.

Mona grinds her butt into the ashtray.

Did you hear me?

Yeah, I heard you.

Okay, says Chesler. He sips his drink.

Mona finishes hers.

Polonsky takes a long drag. Daisy watches Mona fiddle with her empty glass. Are you hungry, dear? she says.

I'm fine, says Mona.

You're looking thin.

I'm fine.

She's so small, says Polonsky. Appetite of a bird.

Chesler says nothing.

A bird, says Polonsky.

Daisy stands up, takes the cigarette from Polonsky's lips and tugs Mona by the elbow.

Come on. We can make some sandwiches.

I'm not hungry.

Maybe Chesler is.

Well, let him make the fucking sandwiches then.

What's with the lip? I'm just asking you to give me a hand.

She tugs Mona by the elbow again, harder this time, and the two women walk into the kitchen.

Hey! says Polonsky. Give me my smoke back!

Mona wants to say something to Daisy, but her tongue is three drinks thick so she just glares at the older woman. Watches her struggle to slice bread. Mona takes a deep breath.

I want to talk to you, says Daisy.

I thought you wanted to feed me.

I might stick my fist in your mouth, says Daisy, if you don't shut up a minute.

Mona takes the knife from Daisy. Cuts a wedge of cheese. Daisy lays the bread on plates.

Well, says Mona, what do you want?

I want to know the real score.

Mona holds the knife at her side, olive skin accented white at the knuckles.

Don't dummy up on me, honey. Out with it.

Mona looks down at the floor. This is the real score, she says. Me, Chesler and his big fucking mouth.

It's just words, says Daisy.

I know, but.

But nothing. Listen to me: find out what this guy's got. And then find out how to get it.

Okay.

Simple, says Daisy.

Yeah.

Then we can relax.

Mona looks up from the floor. Yeah, she says.

Eli watches the clock tick tick tick before the old clerk returns with two file folders under his arm, elbow garters aquiver.

Thanks, Lefty.

Unnf.

Eli sits at the nearest table.

The first file contains all the clippings on the city centenary. He rarely reads his own copy, but now he pores over each word, follows every column of print from beginning to end. With all the articles fresh in mind, he opens the second file. Spreads two dozen photographs on the table. Black-and-white pictures of the Fife and Drum Band, Chief Draper, the mayor. Smiles forced and frozen. Next come the crowd shots. Another two dozen pictures of anonymous men and women, samples of teeth and hair and skin. Eli looks these over closely, runs his forefinger slowly across every face until he is touching a bump on the nose. A strand of dark hair. The entire outline of her face.

He stands in the hallway for a moment and looks both ways. Unlocks the door. Inside the room, he hangs up his hat and sees the conical yellow from his floor lamp, the pale light inching across the rug and floor and foot.

Eli loosens his tie. Make yourself at home, he says.

Okay, says Mona.

Eli walks into the centre of the room. Mona sits on the windowsill. Taps her ash outside.

Couldn't find an ashtray, she says.

I don't smoke.

She nods. Pupils shift from one side to the other. His whole home in a glance.

So, she says. You've got something for me.

Yup, says Eli. Just been to the morgue.

Who died?

No no. The newspaper morgue. The file room.

Oh.

He shows her the photo. Sees her eyes blink and widen.

That doesn't prove anything, she says.

I'm not a cop. I don't want proof.

What do you want?

Eli smiles. Show me your stuff.

For an hour, they walk around his room. Slow turns past the coffee table, a pause beside the lamp. A short breath between stillness and movement, then the long rectangular floorboards creak. Every step announced.

Hey, she says.

He turns around. She holds his wallet and keys and a pencil. All the contents of his pocket.

One more time, he says.

Eli feels nothing but her eyes. Her look lambent in all angles of the room. He knows she would recognize him by the shrug of a shoulder, the way he turns his head. He tries to distract her with gesture. Fiddles with the radio, stops in the spot where light falls in the mornings.

Well? he says.

Not yet.

Not yet?

Keep walking.

They continue, in lines intricate and telling, like the whorls of a fingerprint. He is careful to touch everything. Day on a calendar, his damp towel. Thrilled with detail, the way knowledge is contained in so many small spaces. He picks up the pace. Brushes past walls, dodges furniture that sits lazily like old dogs. He jumps over a footstool, with Mona right after him, laughing, never further behind than the tips of her fingers.

When you work a tip, you get hundreds of suckers moving at the same time, she says. I like that. Took me years to learn how they walked, what they did with their mitts. How they hold newspapers and shopping bags.

You have to break things down to a snail's pace, he says.

Mona pulls out a smoke. Taps it.

Not really, she says. The whiz has its own speed. You just got to know how fast to move.

She lights up. Takes a drag.

Ever been caught?

Mona exhales. Smoke cuffs her at the wrist.

Nope, she says.

No record?

Un-uh.

You must be good at what you do.

Mona shrugs.

What about your partner?

Nice try.

What?

I didn't say nothing about no partner.

So you're a single operator?

Didn't say that either.

Eli smiles. Remember, this is all confidential.

Mona shrugs again, but this time she also smiles.

He talks with her the next day and the next. Hears the questions jump off his tongue and into the room, single syllables like *when* and *who* and *why* that suddenly have the heft of tirade. And her languid answers, in a voice that grows deeper into the night. Drags around the vowels.

What was the first thing you stole?

Pack of cigarettes maybe. Or a candy bar. I remember stealing cherries from the market when I was six, seven years old. Not to eat. To throw. Little red explosions all over everyone's front porches.

Eli leans back in his chair. Cup of coffee in his hand.

What about the whiz?

That came later. In my teens. My old man was a station grifter. He turned me out.

Taught you to stall?

Yeah.

What was that like?

Boring. The same thing over and over. Plant your prat. Throw your hump. Worse than school.

Remember your first time on the whiz?

Oh sure. We took a young guy. Kind of stooped over like an old man so I had some trouble setting the frame. Pratted him in a little too soon and we had to let him gee.

You mean let him go?

Right. Boy, my old man was mad as hell. Gave me shit that night.

Can't say *shit*.

What?

This is a newspaper. You can't say *shit*.

Oh.

How about *gave you a stern lecture*?

Okay. Whatever.

Where's Mona?

Beats me.

She ain't been around much, says Polonsky. Not since that paper business.

She's in the clear though?

Yup.

The snoop was bluffing?

That's what she says.

Atta girl. She sure knows how to work it.

Hey, says Chesler. Are we here to yap or are we here to play cards?

Cards, says Levitz.

Cards, says Slotsky.

Good, says Chesler. Queen high. Still your bet, Slotsky.

Slotsky tosses more chips into the middle. Polonsky follows. Levitz does not move.

You in or out? says Chesler.

Levitz still does not move. With his head shrunken onto his round shoulders, he looks like a man in perpetual shrug. He scratches his chin and stares at his cards. A four and a six. He pushes them aside.

Not enough blood for me, he says.

The phrase, says Slotsky, is *too rich for my blood*.

Whatever, says Levitz. I'm still out.

Fine by me, says Chesler, who tosses his own chips into the middle. Then he deals the next card.

Well well, says Slotsky. He has a pair of queens showing.

Two ladies, says Chesler. Two goddamned ladies.

Slotsky shoves a handful of chips into the pot and waits.

Polonsky squints at his cards. A ten, an eight and a three. Well?

Nah, says Polonsky and he folds his cards.

Chesler jingles a pair of chips in his hand. His fist tightens.

Just you and me, says Slotsky.

Yeah, says Chesler. He looks at his cards. Two, six and seven. His head bobs slightly, his hand taps the table. He stays in the game.

A tidy little pot, says Slotsky. A nice chunk of change.

Chesler deals one more card face up. Slotsky holds at two queens. Chesler stares at his pair of twos.

Still your bet.

Slotsky adds only a single chip. I'll go easy on you, he says. Your luck's taken a bad turn.

Fuck, says Chesler.

You in or out?

Fuck.

Early one evening she knocks at the door. He opens up. Into the room she comes, shrugging out of her jacket. An arm vanishes into the lining and emerges with three plums and two oranges. Mona piles the fruit into a bowl on the table.

Eli watches from the door. Hands on hips.

Didn't expect you today.

Mona shrugs. Sits. Pocketed these on the way over, she says.

Eli smiles. Still off the whiz?

Yeah.

For how long?

Mona shrugs again. She peels an orange. Pulls free an eighth of the fruit and puts it to her lips. Eli walks over and reaches for a plum.

Must've been a big score, he says.

Biggest in a while. Lot of two-dollar pokes in this town.

Ever take it on the road?

Nah, says Mona. Big hassle. Especially for me. 'Cause the stall's got to be the steer on the road.

Steer?

Yeah. The one who figures the trains and where to flop and which dicks are good for the fix. Got to cover every wrinkle.

I see.

Some guys love that action. Working the angles all the time, but then when do you enjoy the dough?

Eli takes a big bite out of the plum.

That stuff's not for me, says Mona. I'm strictly a local gal.

Eli wipes juice off his chin.

Rip and tear?

Clumsy, says Eli. Not a first-class cannon.

Bang a souper?

Steal a pocket watch.

Good, says Mona. Keister kick?

Uh. Hip pocket.

The dipsy?

A warrant.

Centre britch?

Eli flushes. Uh, he says.

Come on come on.

Well, the space between the left britch and the right britch.

The cock, says Mona.

Right. Cock.

You're catching on. How about raust?

Um, says Eli.

Mona jabs his hand with the lit end of her cigarette.

Ow! What was that for?

An example, says Mona. A raust is misdirection. Takes your mind off one thing and onto another. Get it?

Eli puts his hand to his mouth. Sucks his burn. Got it, he says.

Good, says Mona.

She takes a drag. Smiles, and he smiles back. Both of them helpless, unable to hold back for a second even though the warnings are as obvious as crooked teeth. The last thing a writer should do is play word games with a grifter. Nothing he says will stop this horizontal business, and when they finally fuck, he discovers a breathlessness and cursing that absolutely startle the larynx.

Women put to work on the 'whiz'

Many of the teams of pick-pockets, or 'whiz' mobs, working the streets of Toronto employ women as well as men, sources say.

'Sure, there's plenty of women on the whiz, and if you ask me, there'll be plenty more,' said one veteran pick-pocket who was interviewed under careful anonymity as part of the Star's continuing exclusive investigation into this sneaky and artful racket.

'Whiz' mobs rely on a strict division of labour. The thief responsible for removing the wallet from a pocket, or 'pinching the poke,' is called a 'cannon.' However, insiders say this is the easiest part of the 'touch.' The more difficult task falls to the 'stall,' the mob member who manoeuvres an unsuspecting 'mark' into a vulnerable position.

'Just a little shove here and there,' said one old-timer. 'You don't do anything to draw attention to yourself. Just hold your mark in one place long enough for your partner to do his job.'

The most common method is for a 'stall' to push with his shoulders and elbows. But a woman 'stall' can use more feminine distractions to get a victim's mind off his money.

'We sure have our uses,' said one 'whiz moll.'

The precise nature of teamwork on the 'whiz' is carried out via coded instructions, or 'offices,' between members of the mob. 'Offices' can take the form of a cough, a whistle or even short, declarative words such as 'stick' or 'cop.' Veterans of the 'whiz' say the victims never catch on to the scheming commands. 'We can kibbitz right there in front of the sucker and he don't even notice.'

Hands blue-veined and small clear away two plates, three forks and a butter knife. Bert Murneau mumbles thanks into a mouthful of peach cobbler. He watches the busboy rattle away and takes a second bite without swallowing the first.

Eli, coffee in hand, pulls up a chair.

Morenz.

Bert.

Bert lifts his fork. Good cobbler, he says.

Hmm.

Did you try the rhubarb yesterday?

No.

So-so.

Eli looks down. Steam twists out of his cup.

What the hell is rhubarb anyway?

I don't know, Bert.

A fruit? A vegetable?

I don't know, says Eli. Listen. Why'd you want to see me?

Bert slaps the noon edition on the table. Upside down, Eli can see that the paper is folded open to his story.

This was supposed to be in the early edition, Morenz. Not the nooner.

I know.

Bad sign. Busting a deadline.

I know.

Any trouble?

No. Nothing like that. Just took a little longer to dig this one up.

Bert looks at Eli. Chews.

Really?

Yeah.

Yeah?

Yeah, I said.

Okay, says Bert. Because you're really getting the goods.

Eli hides his smile behind a sip of coffee.

Can you keep milking it?

I guess so.

Because the boss is lapping it up. Real razzle-dazzle, he says.

Okay.

He says there's even some pressure hitting the boys at headquarters. A little heat on the cops to catch some of these guys.

Really?

Oh yeah, says Bert. We may have something real good going.

Eli takes a big gulp of coffee. He looks down into his cup. Watches a beige drip on the china blear and run.

There was the time, she says. The, uh, time when I framed this dick. A wrong copper. He'd, um, he'd been putting the shake on us for, for. Uh.

Eli lifts his mouth from between her legs and says, Can't this story wait?

And the time this sucker grabbed me and was gonna beef gun unless I gave him a tumble.

Really? says Eli.

Mona licks the perspiration off his sternum.

Yup, she says.

What'd you do?

She slides up so they are face to face in his bed. Brushes a strand of dark hair behind her ear.

Played along. Took his arm and told him I'd make it worth his while if he stayed hush-hush.

And?

And he bought it. Took me to this place he knew.

And then you gave him the slip, right?

No no. I let him fuck me. Then he fell asleep and I grabbed his pocketbook on the way out. The whole deal lasted half a minute.

Eli looks at her. I don't think I can print that, he says. How about another?

Mona rolls onto her back. Eli keeps his eyes on the outlines of her body. Dark pubic triangle situated in the white rectangle of the bed. She is framed in the sheets.

Sheesh, she says. You're just like the whiz. Always after something.

Yeah, says Eli. But in my business, we don't just take. We also give. We give our readers exactly what they want.

Three days later, a mouth of men in bad suits tightens around Staff Sergeant Joe Goss. A tall man with a walrus moustache crushed between a creased brow and two chins. He clasps his hands together and waits while flashbulbs bite and the press begins to feed piece by piece.

So, says Oliver of the *Globe*. You're the big whiz copper.

Yes, says Staff Sergeant Goss. I head the new pickpocket squad.

Any plans on how you're going to handle the whiz mobs?

Some.

Know where they hide out? asks Thornley of the *Telegram*.

We can guess.

Some people say pickpockets are the worst racket there is, says Arthur of the *Mail and Empire*.

Is that a question?

The insistent brightness of the flashbulbs makes Staff Sergeant Goss glare. He shields his eyes from one more burst of light and hears a reporter laugh.

Are they a menace? says Eli.

To personal property they are, says Goss. I don't believe any of them are dangerous.

There's a lot of them out there, though, says Gow of the *Star*.

Yes.

How many men are in your squad?

As many as can be spared.

What if that's still not enough?

Where the lion's skin will not reach, you must patch it out
with the fox's.

Who said that?

Plutarch.

Plutarch?

Yes.

Is that one T or two?

Part Three

May 1934

In the press room of Police Headquarters, Gow, Thornley, Arthur and Oliver compare coverage of a raid on a bookie joint in the Junction. Huddled over splayed newsprint, the quartet chirps at any dichotomous fact.

Melee, says Gow, tapping the open page of the *Telegram*. There wasn't any melee. All they did is knock over a mutuel machine.

Thornley shrugs. I like that word, he says. It's got good colour.

I like *fracas*, says Oliver. Or *brouhaha*.

How about *rumpus*?

Hubbub.

Skirmish.

Two seats over, Eli reads the occurrence sheet. The daily list of arrests is cluttered with common violations – labour protesters and public drunks – but lower down the page he sees a small crowd of familiar names. Lewton, Vigo, Hashmall. Two cannons and a stall, whiz veterans whose inherent shiftiness has landed them on a police blotter.

How about *donnybrook*?

Or *fray*?

How about dropping it, says Gow.

You brought it up, says Thornley.

All I said is you're making a small story sound big.

Look who's talking. At least my paper isn't spilling all this pickpocket nonsense.

Geez, Thornley, you've written your share of stretchers before. If Morenz says there's more to the story, then there's more to the story. Right, Morenz?

Eli stands up quickly.

Right, he says.

He walks down the front steps of Headquarters, then west on College. Heading home. Late-afternoon edition in his hand, but little zephyrs flap the pages so he stuffs the paper under his arm and loosens his tie.

Augusta, Bellevue, Lippincott. Block after block, the wind picks up, welcome breeze on a warm day that blows litter around his feet and then flips his hat off his head. Flops it along the sidewalk. Another gust shoots the hat across the shoetops of five pedestrians before Eli puts the grab on his brim just beside the shop of F. Merkle Dressmaker. He holds his hat lightly. Straightens up and, staring at the window display of a judy's bosom, he reflects.

Behind the slatted door of the fitting room, Mona slowly disrobes. Layer after layer falls away, the impression of her fingers barely lingering in the discarded fabric. She reaches for a hanger. Studiously works the eye and hook on an ecru skirt, the buttons of a red-and-white spotted blouse. Small gestures of the hand so different from when she is on the boost. No flow in this cramped space, nowhere to channel the instinct that runs rampant on the whiz. Here, the limbs and motion of others are partitioned off. She can hear the chatter of women down the corridor. Imagines the pale flesh that hangs off their arms, like old linen on a clothesline. Mona adjusts a strap over her bare shoulder and turns toward a knock at the door.

Need a hand in there? says the Simpsons salesgirl.

No, says Mona. No thanks.

Holler if you do.

Okay, Mona mumbles. She takes a swallow of air. Buttons up. The boosted blouse fits so snugly under her own clothes that · she can exit the store without a wrinkle.

She affects a stroll on Queen. Tight gait loosens with every step on the busy sidewalk. Easily dodges a street sweeper and a couple holding hands, passes storefronts with corbelled brick and oriel windows. St. Patrick, McCaul, Beverley. Street signs to billboards, her eyes widen with the size of letters. SMOKE CHESTERFIELDS. No cigarettes left, nothing to do with her hands, so she stashes them in her pockets and keeps moving. Lost in thought when she bumps a man on the beat.

Oooops.

Sorry.

She stands shoulder high. Looks up slowly at badge, then jaw. In the seconds it takes her to form a smile, she could steal his handcuffs, the nightstick off his belt.

My fault, she says.

The officer excuses himself with a tip of the hat.

No problem, miss.

Mona takes it on the heel. Continues west, but makes the first turn north that she can.

Well, says Mona, what do you think?

Uh, says Eli.

Too splashy?

No no. I like it.

He holds up the tie, yellow silk with a string of maroon triangles down the middle. Across the table, Mona furrows her brow. Thumb and the first two fingers of her left hand try to tie a shoelace. She manages to make the two bows.

Thanks, says Eli.

Mona shrugs. I was grabbing some stuff anyway.

Boost?

Yeah.

Which store?

What's with the questions? You writing about shoplifters now?

Eli shakes his head. One racket at a time, he says.

Mona looks over. Holds his eyes while her fingers continue to move. Between the middle digit and the ball of her thumb, she slips one bow under the other and then the index finger pulls the knot tight. She lifts the aglet. Dangles the shoe.

Ta-da!

Eli applauds. What else have you got?

With slow continuous pressure, her mouth moves from his belly gone hollow with inhale up to a nipple, sternum, chin. He utters only a syllable before her tongue circles in answer. Around and around in his mouth. Her hand steals away from the small of his back. Lolls along the thigh. Fingers his asshole.

Uh, says Eli. That's not my pocket, you know.

Who's the grifter, chum?

She laughs. Him too. And then minutes later, despite their stentorian fucking, he can still hear her words in his head. The phonetic echo of them rattling around after he comes, so she remains inside him even as he pulls out of her.

Chesler, Slotsky and Levitz sit in the Roxy Burlesque after a long day at the track. Whiskeys all around. Their table is close to the dark, circular stage where a piano player lurches cadaverously over the keys. Plink plunk goes the piano. Plink plunk. Levitz pokes Slotsky with his finger.

It was the mud.

Sure sure, says Slotsky.

I'm telling you it was the mud, says Levitz. You could see it in his eyes.

You saw it in his eyes?

Yeah.

So why'd you bet on him?

Shit, I didn't know it at the time. He was five-to-one. I had a hunch.

A hunch?

Yeah.

No hunch about the mud?

Shit, who has a hunch like that? Two steps out of the gate and he's got a view of the field.

The ponies'll kill you. Every time.

Chesler sips his drink.

That's not all, says Levitz.

No? says Slotsky.

Nope.

Levitz pokes Slotsky again. Somewhere near the quarter, he says. Just ups and bucks the jockey. Right in the air. Landed in a puddle. Boom.

Wow, says Slotsky. Where is he now?

Now? Where do you think? The glue factory.

No no. The jockey.

Oh. I don't know. Hospital, I guess.

That's terrible.

You're telling me. I had a ten-spot riding on him.

Another sip for Chesler while a woman sashays across the stage. Scant applause in the glare of sequins. Tassels and a feather boa and then one long leg extends over the back of a chair. Chesler downs the rest of his drink and orders another round. He slaps Slotsky lightly on the shoulder.

Spot me on this one, he says.

Morning. Showered but still bleary-eyed, Eli knots his new tie on the way down the stairs. He yawns. Exits the side door of the smoke shop and runs right into McMaster.

There you are! says McMaster.

Here I am.

Been looking for you.

Eli looks up. McMaster smiles down, then drops a big mitt onto Eli's shoulder.

Let's go, chum.

Forgive the impromptu meeting, Morenz, but I've been eager to chat with you for quite some time. Busy schedules such as ours often require a little improvisation, eh?

Staff Sergeant Goss leans toward the driver's seat and taps McMaster on the shoulder.

Star Building, Mac.

Okay, boss.

McMaster's big hand palms the wheel as he steers the police sedan into traffic. Goss resettles in the back seat beside Eli. He purses his lips, leading his walrus moustache and double chin in a syncopated twitch.

Now then, he says. I've been reading your work. Impressive, Morenz, most impressive. In less than two months, you've managed to sway public opinion. To influence the decision-makers. The whole town is scared of pickpockets. You, of course, know better. So do I. Pickpockets are a mere nuisance. Nothing more, nothing less. Unfortunately, the chief and his political masters believe everything they read, and so the end result of your stories is a hasty rearrangement within the department. No longer am I a staff sergeant down at HQ. No. Now I'm called upon to chase down these small-timers in the street. Me! After nineteen years! Feh!

Eli writes everything down, the scribble in his notebook not stopping until the moment Goss grabs away the pencil.

Eli looks up. No rough stuff, he says.

Of course not, says Goss. I just don't believe our conversation is suitable for publication.

Background?

Goss nods.

Okay, says Eli.

Understand, Morenz. I don't blame you for any of this. You have your papers to sell and I respect that. Crime, for your readers, is entertainment. But for me it's a business. And because of this business, I have to approach all matters with great heed. I can't have my men running around the city willy-nilly. Brawn is clearly not the answer here. No, Morenz, we need to take a more careful, certain path to success.

We?

Of course we. Who else shares the same goal? Once this so-called Centenary Mob is put away, you'll get your scoop and I'll get back to where I belong.

What am I supposed to do?

Goss sighs.

College man, aren't you, Morenz?

Yeah.

Five years at the newspaper. City beat. Now you're a police reporter?

Sort of.

Well, here's something you'll need to learn about this kind of news game: your people and my people often exchange information. Perhaps a name. Perhaps an address. Any tidbit that might help us clear up this foolishness.

Nothing comes to mind.

Well, it will. I have no doubt it will.

I get you, says Eli.

Good, says Goss. I knew you would. And Morenz?

Yeah?

I like your tie.

The sedan pulls up beside the Star Building. Eli gets out. Says nothing. Stuffs his hands in his pockets and turns. In two steps, he is part of a crowd that pushes through the front doors, click-clacks across the marble floor and squeezes into a waiting elevator. Shoulder to shoulder with the composing-room foreman on one side and a familiar stenog on the other, Eli mutters not even a hello as the doors begin to close.

Pickpocket squad a 'success'

The city's new pickpocket squad has become a constant scourge of wallet-grabbers since its inception 10 weeks ago, according to the man in charge of the 'whiz' cops.

In an exclusive interview with the Star, Staff Sgt. Joe Goss said pickpocket crime is already way down. 'I haven't seen any numbers yet, but I can assure you that arrests are up. Pickpockets are not the bravest lot I've encountered, and once they learn this type of crime is no longer tolerated, then my guess is they'll move on.'

The latest 'whiz' arrest came at the Edward St. Bus Terminal. Morris 'Moe' Hashmall, of Grace Street, was charged with jostling two nights ago. 'This is exactly the type of long-term transgressor we want to put away,' said Staff Sgt. Goss. 'And once we grab this so-called Centenary Mob, we can call ourselves a complete success.'

Staff Sgt. Goss was quick to direct credit to an unlikely source. 'The press has publicized our plight as much as possible. We're all aware of the situation. Now we're keeping our eyes peeled.'

Mona opens the door. Quietly pads through the vestibule and up the first three stairs before she hears the crash of glass and a string of curses from the living room. She doubles back. Sticks her head around the corner.

Daise?

Daisy stands beside the radio with an empty bottle in her hand and two broken ones at her feet. Loose strands of hennaed hair clash with the pink that flirts in her face.

Fucking mitts, she says.

Mona grabs a broom from the kitchen and when she returns, Daisy, on the divan, is massaging her hands.

Fucking mitts, she says again.

Mona starts to sweep. In the straw of her broom are large shards, glistening bits.

Some night, says Mona.

Tell me about it. Poor Hashmall.

What do you mean?

Hashmall. Cops dropped tin on him yesterday.

Shit!

You didn't hear?

No, says Mona.

Guess you've been busy.

Mona tightens her grip on the broom handle.

You think I don't know you've been stepping out?

Mona stops sweeping.

Sheesh, honey, don't give me that look. A little action's just what you need right now. Keep it up.

Mona turns to leave.

Where're you going? says Daisy.

Bed. I'm bushed.

You won't get much rest. Chesler's there.

What?

He passed out last night. Took three of us to lug him up the fucking stairs.

To my bed?

Daisy shrugs. Knew you wouldn't be using it.

Well well, says Chesler.

Mona stands in the doorway. Hands on her hips.

Chesler lies, fully clothed, on her bed. Scratches his stubbled chin.

Mona walks into her room and opens the window. A waft of outside air is quickly subdued by manstink and the odour of stale cigarettes, the lifelong reek of this racket. She grabs the ashtray and empties it out the window.

Where've you been? says Chesler.

None of your fucking business.

Hear about Hashmall?

Yeah.

Fuck.

Mona sits on the windowsill. Taps the ashtray lightly against her palm.

We was passing the sheet last night, says Chesler. Get a little dough together for his wife.

Okay.

I put us down for a C each.

Okay.

But you'll have to cover me.

What?

I'm busted.

Cards or horses?

Both.

Mona looks Chesler in the eye for ten long seconds, then turns her back to him. Her hands dip into the clutter on her bureau, tossing off an old newspaper and a deck of cards and even some loose change.

So we're back on the whiz? she says.

Course. Don't tell me you're shy all of a sudden.

Mona turns around again with a cigarette in her mouth. She strikes a match.

I ain't shy, she says.

So you're ready?

Mona shoots out a long, twirling line of smoke.

Sure I'm ready.

The dispatcher's garbled voice spits out of the radio at Police HQ. Thornley, Arthur and Oliver circle the machine, their faces blank and pale. Every second of static is a scoop lost. When the next call comes through, the trio takes action. Thornley slaps the side of the radio, Arthur and Oliver chuckle.

Gow, sitting on the edge of the desk behind them, chuckles too. He turns to Eli, who chews his pencil over the mid-morning *Star*.

Anxious, Morenz?

Eli looks up. About what?

Page one. Some guys get a taste of it and start stewing over how to stay there.

Eli shrugs.

Not that you don't deserve it, says Gow. Did a nice job dressing up all that legwork. Real nice. But how far can you take it? Can you point a finger at these yeggs?

Eli takes a deeper bite on his pencil.

Because if you can do that, Morenz, you've got the makings of a real dick in you.

On the departures concourse of Union Station, Mona moistens her lips so the paper of her cigarette does not stick. She walks and smokes, walks and smokes. Passes three swells bossing around a redcap, then a dame and her poodle and, finally, a big cop alert in the middle of the tip. Mona keeps moving. By the time she has smoked the cigarette down, Chesler has given the office. She reverses position and comes through, just to the right of an old bates. Chesler steps in from the left, on a sharp angle, and comes away with a flat wallet from the breast pocket. Their first score in weeks.

Mona plants her prat against another mark. Chesler, beside a right coattail, slips his duke just under an elbow and lifts up the flap of the pocket. He puts a pinch on a city map folded to the same size as a wallet.

The next mark gestures with his newspaper. His two friends nod and light thin cigars. Twin fires. From bowlers to brogans, the friends identical in every way except they smoke with opposite hands. They inhale at the same time and both lean over to sniff the white carnation in the mark's lapel. The mark laughs and continues to wave his paper around.

Two steps back, to the right, Mona watches.

The mark makes a slight bow. The twins tip their hats and laugh as one. Backslaps and handshakes and then they separate. The mark moves one inch forward in the crowd and two sideways, a pause and shuffle through the men's-room lineup before being bogged down near a newsboy. In the dawdle, Chesler grows very deliberate. Gauging a slight limp in the mark, he readies his own hip and waist. Gets set to mimic a stride that falls heavy on the right. The pace picks up again. Chesler is in perfect step. He fans the mark in five seconds and offices for a left britch score.

Mona is in position. Her elbow grazes the mark's forearm, her back braced and limber. She plants her prat. Feels the man behind her, his hesitation. Chesler, closer now, inches the tips of his fingers beside the pants pocket and collects a little dope on the way. Stubble on the nape means a recent haircut. A sharp dresser too, fussy and clean, so there'll be a lack of body oil in the clothes. Makes a roll of bills tough to reef. Chesler takes pleat after pleat, the seconds moving slowly, the roll almost in his palm when he sees a muscle pound in the neck and he knows he has rumbled the mark. He lets go and falls back a step, another step, until he is safely in the crowd, glaring and empty-handed.

The day is chased away by dusk, the sun a bloodshot eye over the horizon. They face each other on the floor, bottles of beer trapped between them. Mona takes a swig. Her blouse is unbuttoned.

So, how was it?

What?

The whiz.

Oh. That. It was okay.

Been a long layoff, says Eli. How's your timing?

Mona shrugs.

No rumbles? No beefs?

Mona says nothing. In the deepening dark of the room, she watches the shadows drift across his shoulder and arm as he searches for something on the floor.

What're you fishing for?

Pencil, says Eli. I should be getting this stuff down.

Can't keep doing this.

Eli turns around, pencil in hand. Doing what?

This, says Mona. Using everything I say. There's enough heat on us as it is.

I haven't spilled anything. No clues about who you are, where you work. I don't even know the name of your partner. I stopped asking.

I know. I know that. But every article you write just makes it worse and worse. There's more cops around the station than ever.

I have to give them something, says Eli.

I know. I just, says Mona and then stops. Her hand flutters uselessly in the air. I just don't want to talk about this anymore.

Eli sips his beer. He looks at Mona. Mona looks away.

The next morning, she rests one foot on a chair while she rolls up her stocking. Along the calf and over the knee, the fabric slowly slips over her skin. Eli, in the bed, watches. Her back to him now. She slides on a navy blouse and begins to button it up. Between her black hair and blue top, the back of her neck appears stark.

Eli yawns.

Mona puts a cigarette in her mouth, but does not light up. Crumples the empty pack in her hand.

Gotta go, she says.

She grabs her coat and walks through the room. Her hand twists the knob. The latch is quietly released. Eli sits up and stares at the closed door.

His fingers curl around a cup of coffee. He takes a sip. Feels a dull ache behind the eyes and at the bridge of his nose, and when he lifts his cup the dullness moves with him. Forging new routes of anatomy. The busboy at the Bowles Lunch rattles past his table, clack clack clack go the dirty dishes. Leftover cutlery clatters in a washbin. Wheels of the bus squeal along the floor, the squealing subdued once they enter the kitchen. Eli hunches over his coffee, the steam twisting into smaller and smaller shapes. He yawns. Late for work. Tired excuses tumble out of the slow motion of his mind: early-morning interview or late-night hunch. None of it matters as long as the copy hits the desk, so he pulls out notebook and pencil and with shaking hands starts a yarn.

Whiz a 'pretty dull racket'

Pickpockets are the least dangerous members of the underworld, one veteran of the lowly profession said yesterday, even as the city's 'whiz' cops were out in full force.

'Why all the fuss?' asked the thief, speaking under condition of strict anonymity. 'We never hurt no one. Sure, we snatch a few wallets now and then, but it's strictly small-time. Any bookie on a slow day clears more than we do in a week.

'We're a pretty dull racket.'

The life of a pickpocket is far different from that of criminals in popular entertainment. The real-life thieves work regular hours, much like ordinary wage earners, even to the point of maintaining the same schedule as honest citizens. 'Whiz' mobs tend to stick to a routine and often do not stray from the city street that is the place of their nefarious business.

The thief said that the sight of city 'whiz' cops does not make the job impossible, only more difficult. 'We always have to sneak around anyway. No one wants a fight. If you pop a knuckle or even get a hangnail, you can't work. There isn't much bang-bang in this business.'

A reedy man with a cardboard grip and the sallow look of a lunger passes Mona and coughs. Coughs again, a tubercular hack that reverberates high in the vaulted ceiling of the Great Hall and disturbs the long-learned cadence of Chesler. Deep in the tip, these reverberations drown out small talk and snickers and every hushed office. Twice Mona plants her prat and twice she awaits word of the poke. She alters her stride, ready to come through one more time when the lunger lets loose with such momentous force he has to spew into his handkerchief. Near the departure ramp, Mona prats herself out. She skulks toward the exit, lugging an uneasy hunch.

A slow night at Daisy's. Drinks doubled up in the lull. Slotsky sits across from his girl, jokes sloshing in the mouth. Daisy and Polonsky recline, with patches of lamplight, on the divan. Polonsky taps the last of the tobacco onto the rolling paper. Thumb and big fingers shape a cigarette. Daisy offers him a match, and over the hiss of the flame she hears the front door slam.

Because I said so! says Mona.

Shaddap!

No! You're gonna do what I.

Fuck you!

Heads turn as Chesler stomps into the room.

Chesler, says Polonsky. What's the rumpus?

Guess!

Polonsky shrugs. Daisy inhales some smoke. Stands.
Exhales.

She is struck by the disorder of her room. Crumpled newspapers
and discarded hose cover the floor. Bent matchsticks float in a
half-glass of beer. In the middle of her bed, an ashtray overflows
onto a game of solitaire. Mona makes a beeline for the pillows.
Tosses them off. Peels away a corner of the sheet. Pulls. Out of
the billowing fabric comes the clank of the ashtray and the seven
of hearts and a shower of grey flakes.

Finished yet?

Mona whirls. Daisy, in the doorway, juts her chin. 'Cause I
ain't cleaning this up.

Mona keeps her mouth shut. Molars clash deep in the jaw.
She sits on the edge of the bed. Daisy walks into the room.

This ain't the first time you've had a spitting contest with
Chesler.

This is different, says Mona.

Why? You guys going busto?

No. Yeah. Shit, says Mona. I don't know.

Maybe you should move around for a while. I can set you up
with some quality gals I know.

I don't know, says Mona again.

She lowers her eyes. Rubs her temples until her fingers
change direction and churn through her dark hair instead.

I'm in trouble, Daise.

Daisy sits beside Mona.

Remember that reporter? says Mona. The one covering the
whiz?

Yeah.

Mona opens her eyes. Stares at Daisy. Daisy's eyebrows jump. Her body follows.

For fuck's sake!

It just happened.

And all this time you've been feeding him the dope?

Nothing big.

Daisy sits back down. Lightly pats Mona on the forearm.

Honey, she says. What were you thinking? Don't never mess with a regular sucker. They're just poison.

I know.

Card player, tout, any other hustler if you got to, but never ever a swell.

I know, Daise.

Honey, you gotta call this thing off.

I know.

I know you know, says Daisy. She pats Mona's forearm with more vigour, her bracelets chattering like teeth.

The room bleeds moonlight. Flecks of it on his bare legs as he paces through the long, awful night. Insomniac eyes stick to his silhouette, the distended limbs that creep, like minutes, past table and chair. Eli stops. Opens his mouth. Even in the dark solitude of his room he says nothing. The last time this mood came on he could hide in the silences, but now he curses the garrotte of language. All the things unsaid slowly strangling him. Eli sits on the bed. He rolls onto his stomach. Buries his face in the pillows.

KNOCK KNOCK.

Eli rolls over. His cock, briefly hard, goes soft. He blinks.

KNOCK KNOCK.

He props himself up on an elbow. Rubs his eyes.

KNOCK KNOCK.

He stands. His body is pale, freckled, confused. He takes a step. Stops.

Mumbled curses on the other side of the door are followed by the steady fade of feet. Seconds later, a door slams below. Eli at the window watches the police sedan circle away from the smoke shop and drift down the dark empty street.

Another slow day on the whiz. She stands in the shadow of the departing streetcar and cuts into Kensington. Chesler is already there. He licks his thumb and finishes counting the bills.

Twenty-six, twenty-seven, twenty-eight.

That's it? says Mona.

We'd have more if you could hold a fucking frame.

That peeper was angling my way.

Uh-huh.

He was.

You had plenty of time.

Mona grabs her share out of his hand. Says something barely audible.

What was that? says Chesler.

Mona walks away.

Chesler, once home, fashions quite a thirst. He pours a shot of whiskey and paces around the room, the shot glass small and hard in his palm. Whiskey burns while once-nimble fingers stumble with buttonholes. He gets his sleeves rolled up, then tears at his tie, the knot at his throat.

Fuck, he says.

He manages only to loosen the knot and walks across the room to the mirror. His face thrown back at him. He sees lines of age that can only imitate expression: a frown, a grin. He looks at himself from several angles, this inexplicable puss. His whole life has been within the strains of grift, his entire livelihood limited not by his reach but by his grasp. He drinks and stares and drinks. He can size up other men in a glimpse.

Back on the street. A furious pace over a short distance leaves her deaf to car horns and the sideways mutterings of dislodged pedestrians. Streetlights go red green red. Sidewalks veer. The whole way, she walks intense and distracted, intuiting herself around every obstacle until she opens the side door of the smoke shop, goes up the stairs and down the hallway to the last door on the right.

Once inside, she looks around his room. The smallness of this space, four walls and a window that collapse around them, her in the doorway and him sitting shirtless at the table. His eyes all over her so of course she strikes a match. The matchstick chars in a blue-orange hiss, goes black and bent between two of her fingers.

She sits down. Blows smoke.

Listen, says Eli. He puts his hand on top of hers, the brief commingling of skins cut short when she pulls away.

Don't, says Mona.

Cigarette paper sizzles loudly in the room. Eli looks at Mona. Says nothing. Each wordless second piles onto the next, the silence of two so much louder than the silence of one.

I, she says.

This, she says.

The cigarette burns low. Ash falls onto the table. Mona watches it without interest.

This is nuts, she says. This is fucking nuts.

She stands up. Walks across the floor and flips the butt out the window. She watches it fall, glow and die. Then a shrug, a small tilt of the head and she turns, takes one step and another and another, and when she nearly has a hand on the doorknob, nearly but has not quite made her escape from this cramped and fetid room, she looks at him once more and says, I.

She swallows. Tries again.

I should.

And then she does.

Lie still.

Lie still.

Lie still.

All he wants is stillness, the absolute freedom from choice. So Eli lets the seconds tick until even that tiny motion resonates in his small room. Forcing him to stir. He picks the sleep from his eyes, sleep that was somehow lodged from a night of wakefulness. He stands. The floor is wonky, deceitful. Each step exhausts him, so he leans on the wall for support. Pulls on his pants. Tucks in his shirt. Angles his hat so the brim limits his peripheral vision and the last thing he notices on the way out is a crack in the ceiling that plunges, like a needle, into the floorboard.

Mona storms down Spadina, smoking cigarette after cigarette rapidly until her throat begins to burn and she stops in a deli for a drink. She sits at the counter, her elbow brushing past a blackboard with the daily special. The old cook turns from a low flame and wipes his hands on a fat-splattered apron.

Yeah?

Coffee.

She listens to two men gossip at the other end of the counter. The clink of cup and saucer, frying-pan sizzle. She stirs cream into her coffee and bumps over the sugar bowl. Granules of white on her fingers. The men watching her now so she reaches into her pocket, fumbles with dimes and nickels, stands up and carelessly empties everything out in front of her.

Further perfidy in the newsroom. His fingers, having lost even their meagre dexterity, sit there. Close enough to the Underwood that the beginning of any word is less than an inch away. But nothing happens. Neither a majuscule nor a minuscule issues forth and Eli curses, the type of guttural spurt that cuts through the drone of clacking keys and makes his neighbour Mackintosh stop and look.

Uh, Morenz?

Fuck!

Morenz? says Mackintosh. You okay?

Eli pokes his forefinger into the machine. Tugs at the ribbon, tugs even harder so he can pull the limp black thing free and, with a flick of the wrist, unspools it through the air.

FUCK!

The whole room absolutely silent now. Out of the phalanx of dropped jaws comes Bert Murneau. Nickel-cigar stub still jammed in the corner of his mouth, his red face getting redder with each tentative step. He lifts his hands like a blessing.

FUCK! says Eli. FUCK! The word shoots, coarse and shuddering, up his throat. Bert comes closer. Eli looks into the typewriter, the paper whiter than orgasm. Bert comes even closer.

Easy, Morenz, he says. Take it easy.

They sit in a quiet King East spot with an old rewrite man named Chaney behind the bar. Reporters from all the papers drop by here, off deadline, to drink – the sole armistice of the circulation wars.

The worst job I ever did was a pickup, says Bert. You know, a picture of the deceased. Some poor fella got knocked down by the Lansdowne streetcar. And only the second day in operation too. Already a killer.

Bert takes a drink.

Anyway, he says. One of them older boys – Kendrick, I think – fingers me for the pickup. I was cubbing then. What did I know? So I dropped in on the widow, all grave and polite, and asked for a photo. Here's the kicker: the widow didn't know she was a widow yet. Not till yours truly broke the news.

Bert shakes his head.

That was my first scoop, he says.

Eli leans on the bar and looks through his empty glass to the other side. He sees his hand. The lines in his palm thick and magnified.

Why are you telling me this?

Christ, Morenz, I don't know. I just want to. I want you to.

Bert gulps his drink.

You know what I want.

Yeah, says Eli. I know.

This isn't about the paper. This is about you. You did a hell of a job on this pickpocket stuff, but how many times are you going to knock yourself out?

Bert's hand moves forward, hovers for a second, then drops carefully onto Eli's shoulder.

How about another?

Okay.

Bert signals for two more. Chaney nods. Smiles. Malicious teeth but a heavy, generous hand. Eli watches one of the glasses get filled. He waits for the second one, waits while time starts to seep, like whiskey over ice.

The side door of Garron's Smoke Shop. Eli, with drunken meticulousness, tries and tries again to fit the key in the lock, but his coordination on this night is boozy and wanting. He stops. Sighs, and over that brief exhalation, he hears an engine being cut. The scuffling of shoes. He turns and sees Goss and McMaster head his way. The two big cops advance casually, side by side, until Goss wiggles a finger and his subordinate stops. Goss keeps coming.

Any tips for me, Morenz?

Yeah, says Eli. Don't drink whiskey on an empty stomach.

Goss nods. The ends of his walrus moustache flick upward, hint of a smile that lurks beneath the lip hair.

Anything else?

Do your own digging.

We are, says Goss. We're digging right now.

Goss halts, an inch away from Eli. Eli looks Goss in the eye, looks but does not see anything beyond his own eyelashes. Glaring inward as the gap between decisions stretches wider, wider, so wide all sense of regret falls away without echo and he is reduced to one small act, the gesture of a lifetime.

He reaches into his pocket.

Here.

He tosses the notebook in the air. Goss catches it, two-handed, against his gut.

Take it.

Goss blinks at Eli, then peers down. Beneath the creased cover, he finds the pages are filled with barely legible pencil. Names underlined and crossed out. Arrows that lead the eye from the top corner to the lower margins. Argot circled with bold question marks. Goss looks up. Starts to say something, then stops.

Up the stairs Eli goes, talking to himself. Crazy mutterings down the hall to the last door on the right. Inside his room, he has barely enough breath to continue, but he does, stringing little baggy sounds together into sentences. He sits in his chair, chin in hand, and lets the jag run itself out. Dozes, off and on, only to startle himself awake with the timbre of his own voice. Sheer repetition like a shot in the arm. He cannot sit still. On his feet at four in the morning, pacing back and forth, the sentences spoken louder now, clear and orderly and without patience, so he leaves his room again. Hustles the length of the hall, down the stairs, and bangs on the door of the first-floor apartment. Five minutes and four curses later, old man Garron, nightcap askew, allows him to use the shop phone.

Eli gets the night man at the paper, sauced and pliable, and shoves his mouth right up to the receiver.

Listen, says Eli. This is Morenz. Yeah, I know what time it is, but I've got something for you. Yeah, it's good. What? No, I don't care what Bert says, just take it down 'cause it's hot, real hot, and I'm giving it to you all wrapped up nice and pretty with a big fat ribbon, okay? Okay. Here we go.

Police close in on 'whiz' mob

The police's pickpocket squad received a tip late last night that they hope will lead to the long-awaited arrest of members of the Centenary Mob. 'This is a good, solid break,' said Staff Sgt. Joe Goss, head of the city's 'whiz' cops.

Staff Sgt. Goss was mum on the nature of the tip, saying only that it came from a well-placed source, 'someone with guilty knowledge.'

The Centenary Mob has been big news for the last two months, ever since a rash of stolen wallets during the city's centenary celebrations created such a public outcry that the police force quickly formed its own 'whiz' squad to address the problem. Pickpocket crime has dropped off significantly since then. Sources close to the criminal 'grapevine' have reported that many local 'whiz' mobs have left town for greener pastures.

'The word is out. Any thief values his freedom more than money,' said Staff Sgt. Goss. 'The capture of the so-called Centenary Mob will close the book on this business once and for all.'

From Front Street they come, hundreds and hundreds who escape the hot morning sun and slip through the massive stone columns of Union Station. Inside the Great Hall, the sun's rays hotter still, redoubling down from clerestory windows so the big heat surrounds them all. A sweltering mosaic. Hustling redcaps criss-cross the floor at oblique angles and a sharp-looking bates brushes off his lapel. Plume-hatted mama, perspiration under the arms, drags behind her one large suitcase and two small boys with itchy pistol fingers. Bang! Bang! they holler, Got you got you! Three feet away, beneath the announcement boards, Goss directs his men with quick juts of his double chin. Uniforms and plainclothes move in accord with the damp jiggling flesh. They wait near the ramp loggia and baggage check, tag behind renitent trippers, the oft-placid people who now shove their way out of town.

Bang! Bang! yells one of the boys. Got you!

Chesler, across from the ticket window, holds the early edition in front of his face. Peeks into the tip. Counts the cops. Half a dozen badges scattered around the floor. Undercover men too – bigger and less oblivious than the regular suckers. Back behind the paper, Chesler breathes deep. Six feet away, the line at the ticket window grows. He spots a right one quickly. Pot-bellied man with bad posture, hat and spine sharing the same slouch. Chesler watches the mark read the train schedule, look at his watch, back at the schedule and then reach inside his coat. Buttons on his vest the size and colour of quarters.

One button undone.

Another button and then one more. A thin wallet pulled out by fat fingers and then Chesler can see two bills shoved between the bars of the ticket window. He folds the newspaper and shifts his weight, sweat dripping down his collar and cuffs.

Attention, passengers. Now boarding, Train 736, with service to Cobourg, Trenton, Belleville, Kingston, Brockville and Cornwall. Please proceed to Track Four. Now boarding, Train 736, with service to Cobourg, Trenton, Belleville, Kingston, Brockville and Cornwall. Please proceed to Track Four.

With whiz dicks all around, Mona ekes out her aggression in small steps. Deftly shuffles in and out, side to side, the pace unaltered despite Chesler's curt office to push it along. Force the flow. She instead slows up, sets the frame on her own time. Shoulders and heat and chatter coalesce on the departures concourse, the scene so ornate that a single incorrect move could shatter everything. Mona, stranded in the incredible stillness, nixes all threat in favour of the mark's belly, suspender and shirt. Chesler again offices for her to stick and finally she does. Slides in front of the mark and plants her prat. Waits and waits and waits while Chesler handles the fan and all the restless peepers blink out from the peripheries.

Bang! Bang! I got you! Got you!

He looks and looks. The tightness around his eyes most telling:
blink and she could be gone. Eli wipes the sweat from his brow,
shuffles left to right and loses costly seconds when a small boy
bangs into him.

Got you! Got yo-OUFFF.

Ungh, says Eli.

Mama. Ma-MAAAAAAAAAAA.

Heads turn toward the cry, but Eli jams himself back-
wards. A slope-shouldered cop veers one way, heat-mottled
redcap the other, and, suddenly, the crowd has resettled. New
contortion that clears the way for a familiar bump on the nose.
Eli inches closer. Sees her glistening profile against a sand-
coloured wall.

Attention, passengers. Final boarding call for Train 736, with
service to Cobourg, Trenton, Belleville, Kingston, Brockville and
Cornwall. Please proceed to Track Four. Final boarding call for
Train 736, with service to Cobourg, Trenton, Belleville,
Kingston, Brockville and Cornwall. Please proceed to Track
Four. Last call for Train 736.

The terminal is all eyes and feet. Mona moves, subtle and lewd,
with Eli right behind her, a witness to all the things she does with
her hips. They ease into a turn. Head toward the departures
ramp, an untold million footfalls having passed this way without

incident. The larcenous moment drags on and on, and Eli, clenched and desirous in anticipation, quickens by half-steps.

He makes his move. Says, Excuse me, sorry, excuse me, sorry, sorry, as he shoves his way forward. An arm's length away, no further than a finger when, with one small swivel of his hips, he bumps into Mona. Breaks up the touch. From this, the tiniest nudge imaginable, an entire commotion bursts free. Screams bound around. Cops rush in, their big hands all over the place. Fuck you, yells a voice. Fuck! A struggle in the crowd spreads out. Eli lurches, loses his balance. Fuck, yells the voice again, and Eli tries to loose himself from the massive stumble. Plants his feet but too late because as far as he can see she is gone gone gone.

Mona runs. Out of the tip and out of the station. Splits the honking autos on Front Street, then the traffic on smaller blocks that swells and dissipates like the air in her lungs. She pants. Takes a turn. Garbage cans rattle, fall, dent her path. She trips on a lid and slams a knee on the way down. Trembling hands splay on the sidewalk, support her while she coughs a two-pack-a-day cough. Spits out something thick. She pants again. Looks over her shoulder.

Twenty minutes of useless invective trail off into thirty more of silence. Chesler, cuffed to a chair, has only one thing to say: I'm not saying nothing.

Goss smiles in the windowless room. He has conducted hundreds of interrogations here, a tight-lipped, airless history that has left the chairs stinking of sweat and the white walls yellow from years of smoke.

Well, says Goss. What do you think of this, Mac?

McMaster, arms folded in a corner of the room, shrugs.

Goss begins to pace. From one end of the table to the other he walks, his stride as slow as the words out of his mouth.

I'm afraid Mac isn't very happy, says Goss. He's a very dedicated officer. Eager as the rest of us for results. Alas, he's also a musician. An integral member of the Fife and Drum, aren't you, Mac?

Yes, boss.

Very dedicated to that too.

Yes, boss.

And rehearsal is when?

Now, boss.

Goss shrinks his stride discernibly, each step smaller and smaller until he is practically at a standstill. He leans on the table. Looks hard at Chesler.

You see our problem. Two pursuits. Both noteworthy. Both simultaneous. Something is going to have to give.

Chesler says nothing.

Goss sighs.

McMaster walks behind Chesler. Pulls a key off his belt and, with a click, Chesler's wrists emerge red on the table. McMaster leans in with big-boned alacrity. CRACK! goes the first finger.

Still, Chesler says nothing. A thin bubble of saliva on his lips.

CRACK! goes the next finger. Chesler slides slowly off the chair, onto the floor, the pain in his mangled fingers raging almost as much as his mean, mean thirst.

She incarcerates herself into the iron tub. Sighs as the hot water surrounds her bones. Mona is hidden by steam; only from the wrists down does she dangle free. She is sore. Sore over the botched job, sore over her bruised knee, the confused blood that grimaces under her skin. Tired eyes seek her knees, sticking like two monuments out of the dirty water. She sinks deeper and deeper and goes all the way under. Keeps her eyes open. They move with sad viscosity from the locked door to the limp towel to the small coins on the bureau that shimmer loosely like small tears. Frail bubbles escape her mouth. Burst in the air. She sits up suddenly and struggles with each short breath, ah-ah-ah.

Eli, at the mouth of Glen Baillie Place, wavers. Spadina babbles commerce behind him, but the alley in front is quiet and empty. He takes the first step, deliberate canter to the unlocked door. Palm on the knob, hinges grate in protest. Further protest is vocal when Polonsky spots Eli inside the house.

Hey!

Daisy jumps in. Without breaking stride, she kicks Eli in the shin.

Ow!

Eli hops on one foot.

In my own fucking place, says Daisy. Fuck!

She gives him another good one before Polonsky manages to get hold of her. She fights, but there is a disparity in the struggle. Her ten arthritic fingers no match for his two healthy hands. Polonsky hoists her, like an old chair, into the next room.

Okay, sweetie, okay.

Fuck!

Eli limps up the stairs. Into her room, where he stumbles in on a game of solitaire. Mona, card in hand and a bottle beside the bed, gasps. Sharp intake of breath charges fitfully down her throat, becomes a vandal in the chest.

Eli stands still. Stares. Five days since he saw her last and the recidivist eye brushes against her bathrobe, thin garment open at the neck and ending at the thighs. He points to the bruise on her knee.

What's wrong with your leg? he says, limping closer.

What's wrong with yours?

Eli shrugs. So much in common, he says.

Mona's eyes rim red. She picks up the bottle and pours. Small drops of whiskey cling to the neck of the bottle and slowly slide down. She watches them hit bottom and then takes a drink.

Breeze, she says. No more scoops for you.

I quit the paper.

Yeah yeah.

I did, he says. Or was fired. I don't really know.

So what do you want now?

Eli limps closer.

I want you to listen, he says. Just listen.

Mona makes a fist. Her fist vanishes into an open hand. She's tight. He holds her hand tight. They talk the night away.

Acknowledgements

Whiz Mob, by the late David W. Maurer (New Haven, Connecticut: College and University Press, 1964), is the definitive work on pickpockets. Like any good thief, I stole from it mercilessly.

The lyrics on page 81 are from Guy Lombardo's 'Don't Blame Me.'

Financial support from the Ontario Arts Council is much appreciated.

Thanks to Stan Bevington, Jason McBride, Christina Palassio and Alana Wilcox.

About the Author

Howard Akler lives in Toronto.

Typeset in Adobe Caslon. Printed and bound at the Coach House on bpNichol Lane, 2005

Edited and design by Alana Wilcox
Cover design by Stan Bevington
Cover photo from the City of Toronto Archives, Series 372,
    Subseries 58, Item 1455
Author photo by Soumen Karmakar

Coach House Books
401 Huron Street on bpNichol Lane
Toronto, Ontario
M5S 2G5

416 979 2217
800 367 6360

mail@chbooks.com
www.chbooks.com